THE
PSYCHOLOGICAL
MOMENT

Robert McCrum has written four previous novels: *In the Secret State*, which was made into a film starring Frank Finlay and Natasha Richardson, *A Loss of Heart*, *The Fabulous Englishman*, and *Mainland*. He also wrote the award-winning television series *The Story of English*. He lives in London.

THE PSYCHOLOGICAL MOMENT

ROBERT McCRUM

First published 1993 by Martin Secker & Warburg Limited,
an imprint of Reed Consumer Books Limited

This edition published 1994 by Picador
a division of Pan Macmillan Publishers Limited
Cavaye Place London SW10 9PG
and Basingstoke

Associated companies throughout the world

ISBN 0 330 33049 7

Copyright © Robert McCrum 1993

3 5 7 9 8 6 4 2

A CIP catalogue record for this book is available from
the British Library

Typeset by Falcon Graphic Art Limited, Wallington, Surrey
Printed and bound in Great Britain by
Cox & Wyman Ltd, Reading, Berkshire

For Elizabeth, Mark and Stephen

Every act of courage is the work of an unbalanced man.

E.M. Cioran

1982

1

I'm going to jump right in at the deep end and admit that I could never have told this story while my father was still alive. What I have to say is a kind of confession and at the same time an act of revenge. He betrayed me. Now I shall betray him. The joke is that he would probably approve. I can imagine the glint of satisfaction and the wicked note of pleasure in his voice. 'I never knew you had the balls, Gilchrist.'

My father liked occasionally to address me this way, as though I was a member of his club. That was our relationship in a nutshell, even in the final days. 'So Gilchrist,' he would say at our rare meetings, relishing my surname, 'how's tricks?' Actually, I now realise, he was at the best of times only a maverick conformist. Sure, you might catch him in his tweeds rolling out of the Athenaeum on a Friday afternoon, flushed with an injudicious brandy, hear him referred to by one and all as 'the Beaver' (an English tag that used to embarrass my semi-American ears), and imagine a pillar of the Establishment, but that, like so much else about him, was camouflage. Only now he's gone am I beginning to come to terms with my mistake.

When I think of those clubs in Pall Mall and those Englishmen in suits, government ministers, Whitehall bureaucrats, newspaper editors, parchment-faced peers, even trendy bishops, cronies all, I recognise that I'm also having to face up to a story that dwarfs my little filial drama, even if, in the last analysis, it seems strangely less important. What my father got up to . . . I will come to this in due course. What Craig Marshall got up to: that is another matter altogether. Until now I have lacked the resolution to commit what I know to

3

paper. Rather than speak out, I have preferred to tolerate the repeated accusations of a man who, in his blacker moments, blames me for everything, even his prison sentence.

The trouble with Marshall is that he's an unreliable witness. Even by his own account he has a taste for fantasy. I'm never sure he knows fact from fiction. But perhaps he's right. Perhaps it was family loyalty that persuaded me to stay silent. Whatever I write now, he'll insist to the end of his days that his conviction for a crime he claims he did not commit is due to an unholy alliance between father and son. That's absurdly far-fetched, of course, but there's no doubt I should have been more cautious at the outset, all those years ago. In my own defence, I have to say that no one has ever successfully challenged the substance of his allegations. The authorities could rubbish him and shut him up, but even now his story retains a potency that is all the more disturbing for its irredeemable murkiness.

I shall never forget the first time I heard that story, in London, one short night in May. I can still picture Marshall's bulky, incongruous figure crowding my hotel room: the satin wallpaper, the half-open minibar, the king-size bed with his incriminating papers scattered across it, and Marshall himself in those heavy black executive glasses so popular at the time. We had the bedside radio turned up loud for security and I remember that song, 'Knowing Me, Knowing You'. We were sitting on the bed. When I wanted to speak to him I had to lean towards him and mouth into his ear. He was wearing a dandyish aftershave, as though en route to an amorous rendezvous. With his suede shoes and heavy tweed suit he was like the straight man in a West End comedy, all the more ridiculous for taking things seriously.

I remember Marshall browsing the room service menu. 'You know, Seymour,' he said, with that peculiar formality of his, 'I think I'd love the States.' He began reciting the names of the cocktails in his attractive Scottish lilt. 'Manhattan, Screwdriver, Rusty Nail, Harvey Wallbanger . . . ' I recall that on this occasion we both settled for a Jack Daniel's on the rocks.

This was in 1977. Marshall's fascination with America was typically passé. He was always slightly out of date, just as he was always inclined to get things slightly wrong.

'In the States,' he said, later that same evening, 'my case would be a cause célèbre. Look at Watergate. That should be our model. Everything's a cover-up here.'

I nodded, only half listening.

'But you will tell my story,' he went on. 'I'm confident of that. You will get things out into the open.'

I did not demur as I should have done. I'd already had a couple, and I regret to say I did not believe enough in his cause, célèbre or otherwise. It was easier to dissemble.

'No problem,' I said. In my crumpled suit and loose tie I must have been the image of the off-duty White House staffer. No wonder Marshall began to press me.

'What I'm asking you to do,' he said, 'is get in touch with the whistleblowers. Woodward and Bernstein. They're the business.'

I remember smiling at his touching faith in the infallible power of the crusading journalist. I tried to put him straight. I knew those guys by reputation. They were chiefly interested in their own back yard.

'Seymour.' There was a melodramatic desperation in his voice, but I put it down to the drink. 'You've got to help me. You're my only hope. Surely you can do something?'

'Sure,' I said. 'I'll talk to the Old Man.'

I was new in my job then. I used to enjoy making that kind of remark. I don't know anyone who did not, at one time or another, hype their role in the U.S. Administration. What Rosencrantz or Guildenstern does not aspire to be a Horatio? I suppose I thought it would keep him quiet. I was nothing if not cynical. After all, I'd only agreed to this meeting thanks to a woman's intervention, and much of what follows starts with the feminine lure. If I had not been in love, none of this would have happened. In retrospect, there's no doubt that Ruth Ritchie was my downfall, my nemesis.

Suddenly, without warning, she was with us in the room, wet-haired and glowing from a swim.

That half smile, that mischievous look: I could never refuse her for long. In memory, she is sexier than ever. In bed, she was tireless, demanding and inventive. She would boast that 'No one roots like Ruth Ritchie', and I, in my innocence, would happily agree. She loved to shout and scream, and would cry out at the apposite moment, arching her swimmer's body. Another fancy was eating in bed. We would order take-out pizzas, spread the food in what she called '*déjeuner sur duvet*', and then return to each other's bodies, our faces slick with wine and oil. I see now that Ruth passed through my life like a hurricane. When the storm eventually subsided I found myself beached here, on Cape Cod, trying to pick up the pieces.

Do I exaggerate? Probably. Hyperbole is my business. I'm a speechwriter by trade. I put words into other people's mouths. Here, for a change, I will abandon ventriloquism and speak, less grandly, for myself.

I was christened Seymour Joseph Lefevre by a Navy chaplain at HMS *Ganges* one raw November morning in 1945. I was named Seymour for my mother's father, a fine corrupt old politician, known throughout the Deep South as 'Sam'. So Sam I became, although my business card announces a certain Seymour J. Gilchrist Jr, for reasons I'll come to shortly. What else can I tell you? I'm just over six feet tall. I have sandy hair, a good complexion and the rangey physique of a long-distance runner. I wear glasses for reading. My star sign is Leo. I am thirty-six.

Recently, I thought I was in the middle of a premature mid-life crisis. To write is to betray and, deep down, I was half afraid it would be myself who was most betrayed. Yet the confusions of experience have become too urgent to be ignored and here, in writing, I hope to find an organising sequence, to make the liberating connection between cause and effect. In my search for a reconciliation with my father's shade, I am putting my trust in what you might call 'the narrative cure'.

2

In anticipation of this moment, I had thought it might be amusing to start with 'Once upon a time', but this is an end, not a beginning, and the more I reflect on what I have to say the more I find, alas, that the lighter moments are few and far between. When I was working in the White House I would boast about living for the present and prided myself on the little humorous touches I'd introduce into the Old Man's speeches. In a word, I was optimistic. Now, stranded like Robinson Crusoe, with time on my hands and the past hanging heavy, I, who have told a thousand half-truths in the service of the great and powerful, must speak honestly for myself.

I hit rock bottom last year. The fall of Eighty-One. Oh boy, was I in trouble! I was living apart from my wife, staying with friends in D.C., sorting out the wreck of a marriage and the wreck of a career. Ruth, now my ex-girlfriend, had disappeared into Europe. Marshall was writing me long, accusing letters from prison in England. My father was dying, and my mother, a few blocks down the street, was trying to wangle me a job with a senator of her acquaintance. My problem was that having worked for the President of the United States, there was only one place to be. But the Republicans were in power, and there was no way I could enjoy the hospitality of the White House commissary in the foreseeable future. It was, as I say, a low point in the life and times of S.J. Gilchrist Jr.

Then, out of the blue, I got this call from Herb Schulz. I've known Herb for donkey's years. I used to say he had the shortest attention span of anyone I've ever known. We worked together in the White House, and before that for the

Democratic National Committee. Our wives played tennis at the same club, our children rode on the same school bus. He had come to Washington in silent pursuit of success, hitched his wagon to the President's train, and when the going got rough stealthily detached himself and headed West. We quit within months of each other, but he was the first to hit pay-dirt. Herb is a genius networker. Soon, he was on LA's inside track, and moving up the field. That's when he got in touch again, so sure of his luck, I suppose, that he felt able to risk lunching with a hard pressed friend.

So one day I had this call. Herb was always the master of the unattributable briefing and his off-the-record habits remain. He will say something like 'Is this line secure?' or 'Are you alone?' After the usual routine, he said: 'I've got it, Sam.' 'What's that?' I said, deliberately obtuse. He paused for effect. 'Willpower,' he said. At first I thought he was criticising me. 'What are you talking about?' I said. 'The bard,' he said. 'Shakespeare In Love.' It was his brainchild and it had, he explained, all the ingredients. Romance. Medieval violence. Poetry. Recognition. I, with my part-English background, would be the ideal writer for the project. 'Besides,' he added, with that old-buddy candour, 'you're cheap.' I was out of work and he knew he was doing me a favour, but I had to resist a little for my self-esteem. 'Asshole,' I said. And that, give or take half a dozen conference calls and a lunch in Beverly Hills, was that.

Herb's agent, who joined us for coffee, toasted the venture as 'an idea whose time has come', but I know the project will never reach the screen. Once I've completed a draft script my troubles will just be starting. When I was in the White House, the golden rule was to stop people fooling with your stuff. In Hollywood, they'll do what they want with my prose. Period. Why should I complain? It's nice to have the work and, frankly, with lawyers' bills, and my ex-wife and kids to worry about, the money helps keep the show on the road.

When I tried to warn Herb of my doubts he gave me

this rap. 'Listen, Sam,' he said, 'there is only one truth about LA.' We were sitting high in a restaurant at the time, drinking cocktails and watching the evening lights of the city below us. 'No one knows anything. No one. You and I,' he went on, 'might as well play poker with this idea. At least when we pitch the script there's a chance that half the guys we talk to will have heard of the subject.'

So I packed a few bags, and came out here to Province-town, taking a lease from the first of January, in the Year of Grace, Nineteen Eighty-Two, as they used to say in the books of my childhood.

The house is hidden at the end of a sandy driveway, looking east across the sea towards the Old World. A wild privet hedge is Nature's Do Not Disturb sign. No one visits, and unless I go to town I see nobody. Among the New Age drifters I can pass untroubled. I have avoided making friends. In a metropolis of two streets, you could end up meeting everyone five times a day. I have come here to work, and to think.

The Cape is an island and not, as many people imagine, a peninsula. It encourages the islander's arrogance. Once, it was the beginning of America, and now it's the end, the ultimate escape. Walk between the soft white dunes, look up into the heavens and feel the sun on your face, and you could be in the Sahara. It's a place that attracts nomads and misfits and people, like myself, who need time to get their heads straight. Those of us who have come here to start again find a naturally recuperative atmosphere, an invitation to make sense of things in solitude and tranquillity.

My routine does not vary. I get up with the sun, at about six-thirty, and take a shower. Then I pull on my oldest, most comfortable clothes, make coffee, light the first cigarette of the day and watch the morning news. If the weather's good I might linger on the deck. Towards eight, I prepare a second pot of coffee to last the morning and go to my work table. I try to stay there until noon, or even one, and sometimes,

10

when I'm on a roll, I'll carry through until two or three. If anyone calls I let the answering machine speak for me.

Each morning I have four hours, maybe five, before I can expect a call from Herb, big, scattered Herb, with his trendy blond ponytail and his personal trainer. His last fad was Royal Jelly, but since his wife left him it's been celibacy. I imagine him getting a wake-up call, climbing into designer sweatpants and jogging along the beach at Santa Monica with his Walkman. Then he'll take a cup of decaf into the den and tackle his roster of East Coast calls, starting with me.

'Hi,' he says. 'How's it going?' I prepare myself for his critique of the pages I've Fedexed the day before. I'm learning to interpret his praise. At first, when he said I was 'doing brilliantly', I imagined he was pleased. I've also learned to suppress any jocularity towards his naïve interjections ('No kidding,' he'll say, or, 'Hey, we're cooking here, Sam') as I elucidate the scarcity of information about the poet. Herb, once famously sardonic, has now become like many other Californians of my acquaintance. He has developed what Ruth used to call 'an irony deficiency'.

When I'm done for the day, I make lunch, usually a light salad, and listen to my messages. Then I go for a walk along the beach, or drive into town to shop and collect my mail. Newspapers, once my addiction, are out. My only luxury is the Sunday *New York Times*. In the evening I make pasta, drink a bottle of good red wine I can't afford, and fall asleep watching television or listening to music. It sounds boring, but strange things happen during those hours in front of the typewriter and I've found that the isolation within has become compulsive.

It is so calm when the wind drops. I look out across the reedy waters of the creek. Beyond the dunes there's the ocean, in all its moods. Here, where the Cape curves like a fish-hook, the Pilgrim Fathers made their landing, but that was in a stormy November. Today, the sea sleeps and the sun is already hot and high, and the wind tickling the sea-grass is

11

scarcely more than a whisper, what Shakespeare might have called a zephyr.

I like it here on my desert island. Beside my desk I have a stowaway's library, my Shakespeare, a Random House dictionary, a second-hand thesaurus and that Gideon Bible.

I have the words on the flyleaf by heart. 'Good luck, Seymour. Revelation I. 3. C.B. Marshall.'

I know what the good book says, yet I cannot bring myself to quote the sentence. There is nothing more annoying than to see a prediction you did not believe in finally fulfilled. Of course, none of it would matter to me if it wasn't for my father's part in the whole affair. Or mine if it comes to that. I thought Marshall was a kind of Malvolio, a tragic figure of fun, but I have discovered to my cost that he is a more substantial character. He has, you might say, finally brought me to book.

So I find myself in the peculiar position of autobiographer and storyteller, and if I seem to hold back a little, from time to time, it's because I am only now coming to terms with the tale I have to tell. Besides, I want to make the most of it.

There's a wine stain next to Marshall's signature, and the date, May 11th, 1977. I suppose we were drunk. I certainly had no idea how, five years on, that dedication would come to haunt me.

Indeed, with Herb's commission in my pocket, I was just beginning to put that part of my life behind me, and to find a new purpose. But then my father died.

12

My father's death, so long expected, was finally quite sudden, a tree falling in the forest. The news that he had gone came unexpectedly when Jane, who nursed him almost to the end, called to share her grief, assuming that the doctor had already telephoned from the hospital. She was confused and lonely, ill at ease with her new responsibilities. The old man had not lost his gift for surprising his nearest and dearest. In death, as in life, the Beaver – as I have to call him – was still the puppet-master. I wondered: did he hope to make us feel guilty by slipping away while we were, so to speak, out of the room?

I was his executor. I closed the house on the Cape for a few days and caught the first plane out. I reached London early the next morning and was down in the West Country by noon. There were primroses in the hedgerows. I had forgotten England's suffocating green.

Until the day of the funeral, a Saturday, I went through the rituals of death alone, consulting no one. My father's life had been conducted like a revel. I felt as though I was a valet, cleaning up the morning after the night before. With so many possible complications, it was easier to take charge and everyone seemed grateful.

I contacted our family lawyer and made an appointment. Then I booked the church, met with the minister, organised a service sheet at a local printer's, paid my last respects in the funeral parlour, and put an announcement in the news-paper. This last duty was not strictly necessary. The death of Admiral Sir Ronald Lefevre, DSO etc., had been widely and entertainingly covered. It is an odd commentary on the British press that some of its best writing should be confined to the obituaries page.

It's amazing how many people read those notices. The jungle drums had been beating. The church was full. Row upon row of distinguished-looking, elderly faces: friends, acquaintances, shipmates, forgotten family, and a mistress or two, small-boned upper-class women with gold on their shoes. I imagined my father scanning the aisles with that involuntary narrowing of the eyes and remarking not so sotto voce: 'Good turn-out, Gilchrist. Well done.'

Mother arrived last, a bride of mourning. I had booked a limousine to meet her at the airport, and she claimed the driver had lost his way, but I suspected it was her wish to make an entrance. I waited while she changed into a pair of shiny black shoes and adjusted her broad-brimmed black hat with the care of a model on location. My mother is what the English call 'a striking woman'. As I escorted her up the aisle, she drew whispered comments on all sides. Taking her place in the front pew, immediately under the lectern, she nodded to the priest as if he were a maître d', and the service began.

I remember the scent of the lilies at the foot of the catafalque and the pale green light, the colour of Sancerre, falling on the heads of the congregation. We sang the English hymns I had grown up with as a boy, before my mother's move to America, 'Father, hear the prayer we offer' and 'Praise my soul, the King of Heaven'. The long, sonorous wash of the Authorised Version rolled through the church. 'All flesh is grass, and all the goodliness thereof is as the flower of the field . . .'

My father was making his last exit in style, as he had wished. He had planned every detail of this ceremony, the Ensign-draped coffin, the Marine honour guard, the Last Post. In death, as in life, he wanted to be in charge, and he was. He used to say that the Navy liked to put on a good show, and they did not let him down.

There was no address.

As soon as it was over, my mother followed the pall-bearers into the spring sunshine. I took her arm. Going towards the west door, I saw faces in the church I had not seen in years. Irreverently, I thought it seemed like an episode of 'This Is Your Life'. Outside, beyond the stone porch, my mother greeted the mourners, some of whom went back to wartime days. Beneath her hat, she seemed very far away.

Jane, who had taken care of my father so faithfully, introduced herself, as we had agreed, and a difficult moment passed off smoothly. Jane had her daughter Susan in tow, a sweet, awkward woman of twenty-something, with too much make-up and the over-bright expression of the mentally disturbed. My mother hardly seemed to notice her and was soon distracted by the sympathies of a retired general.

Mother and I went to the crematorium in the funeral limousine, alone. That was her wish, in fact her only demand, and I had implemented it without too much acrimony. In the Chapel of Rest, stripped of its flowers, the coffin seemed lonely and vulnerable. I took my mother's hand and found my squeeze faintly answered.

At the final moment, as the squeaky automatic curtain drew round the casket, hiding my father from view, I remember feeling suddenly free. A great weight seemed to have been taken away. I felt younger and disloyally light-headed. I watched his widow kneeling in prayer and wondered if I could ever confess this mood. What was she thinking? I would probably never know.

We were due to go back to the house where the other mourners had been invited for tea and refreshments. As I expected, my mother said she did not want to accompany me. Her driver would take her back to London. Tomorrow she would fly home. I did not press her to change her mind. She dropped me at the foot of the drive and kissed me. 'You will know how to handle everything,' she said calmly. 'Come home soon.'

I watched until she was out of sight, and turned to walk up to the house, as dizzy as a child released from school. Jane was on the doorstep to greet me, my father's dog by her side. I explained that Mother had gone back to London, and Jane seemed relieved. People say such odd things at these moments. 'Susan has prepared some delicious salmon sandwiches. She really is much better, you know.' I said I was glad. 'I hope you will let her see the will,' she added. 'It might help her to understand.' She turned away, holding back her tears with difficulty.

Inside, some of the guests had moved instinctively on to the whisky, and the party was beginning to go with a swing, as my father would have hoped. I was introduced to several military men as 'the Beaver's boy'. One or two old hands expressed sadness that Mother had left so soon, but several unfinished sentences hinted at an awkwardness avoided.

As the drinks flowed and condolences gave way to reminiscences, the occasion took on the air of a veterans' reunion. Soon, most of my father's friends were arguing about the Falklands. Almost all regretted they could not see action again, many were afraid that the Task Force was, as one put it, 'too much of a dreadful bloody gamble', and some thought that the government would fall.

'Nice place, Buenos Aires,' said one old codger. 'The Argies play the best polo in the world. It's just those generals who give me the willies.'

4

There is nothing harder to face than the things left by the dead.

Jane could not bring herself to clear my father's room and she evaded the responsibility, persuading herself that it was the executor's duty. I said I would do it my own way, and she must not mind. She nodded dumbly and I went upstairs with a roll of black garbage bags.

I felt like a burglar as I crossed the threshold, but once I was standing on the sheepskin rug by the bed I became a small boy spying on a mysterious, grown-up world. My curiosity was soaring. This was the moment I had waited for. I put out my hand to steady myself. The bedspread was cold. For a moment, I could not move.

There was the smell of sickness and disinfectant in the air, though a fresh April breeze was rattling the open window. Someone had put daffodils on the dressing-table, as if a visitor was expected. I was struck by the defiance of the gesture, the assertion that the world in which daffodils were picked for guest bedrooms, that life itself, went on.

Gradually, my heart returned to normal and I found my resolve. I peeled off the first of the black bags and addressed the wardrobe, catching my pale face in the mirror as the door swung open. My father used to pencil my height against the inside of that door, usually on my birthday. I had reached a long-legged four foot nine when the measurements stopped.

The wardrobe, an arsenal of vanity, bursting with neatly folded clothes, betrayed his double life. As a civil servant, even an unconventional one, he had been obliged to wear subfusc. Out of the office, he had indulged a summery taste in silks, a fin-de-siècle love of velvet. Dozens of neckties told

17

the story of a man who could never refuse an invitation to join a team or a club though he was, in truth, the worst team player you could imagine. Taking the plunge, I began to stuff these peacock feathers into my first bag, piling shirts, socks and scarves higgledy-piggledy on top of embroidered waistcoats and crumpled safari shorts. The charity people could sort them.

Next, I turned to the smaller personal items in the cupboard. I had to tread carefully here. There were family snaps in silver frames to pass on. The record of travel and vacations suggested a deep restlessness. Official photographs recalled the life of a man who could never put his feet up. He had often been at the heart of things. There was that signed photograph of Harold Wilson he'd kept. 'Despite everything, I rather liked him,' he had said to me once.

I turned away. I did not care to dwell on that occasion.

I pulled open musty drawers and found starched collars, studs, medals, silk handkerchiefs and tubes of cream and ointment. Among his medicines and pills there were several packets of condoms, in different languages, together with a box of trout flies.

I cannot deny the satisfaction I found in clearing my father, so to speak, out of the house.

I stacked my black bags in the corridor. It did not take long to dispose of his things. I hurried as fast as I could, oppressed by the futility, driven by the urge to sweep the evidence of his life away. A few items, his ceremonial sword, for instance, I would keep for my son, Charlie, but that was all. In less than two hours, I was sitting at his desk, sorting through his papers.

He had, of course, known that he was dying for at least three years, and he had prepared for that fell rendezvous with systematic care. Everything was labelled. It was as if he was waiting for me. There were a few surprises. A letter for Mother, together with a battered album containing some

18

photographs of the Lake District, and a book of poems, *Other Men's Flowers*.

Finally, there was the will. We had gone over this ground already, some years before. But had he, I wondered, changed his mind?

I scanned the pages quickly. A man notorious in his life for his unpredictable ways turned out in death to be completely reliable. 'Not my style to be caught on the hop,' he would have said. The will was the will I expected, exactly as he had promised.

I was sitting there alone, with this document before me, when the door creaked and Jane's daughter, Susan, came in.

'Hello,' I said.

'Finished?' she said, coming over to my side.

I nodded. I felt awkward, having the will open on the desk.

Then she kissed me like a child and said: 'Can I come to America?'

But Susan is, at best, only half my responsibility. I wanted independence now more than ever. Deep down, I knew the moment had arrived when I could at last begin this story.

I returned to America alone.

When I reached home, as I call it, I wrote Herb to tell him in the nicest possible way that his precious first draft was going to be a month or so late. There's nothing I have to say for myself that can't be put down on paper inside forty days.

5

When I try to analyse the past now it's like meeting an old friend in a foreign city.

A few nights ago, Charlie, who has been visiting here with his sister for a few days, said: 'How's Ruth?' Just like that, a cheerful 'How's Ruth?', as if we were two buddies having a beer and a chat. He's on the edge of puberty and his current life project is to identify my weak points.

I'm sure the little brute had been poking about among the papers on my desk and found the postcard announcing her imminent arrival. 'She's fine,' I said, attempting casualness. A vain hope.

'Do you still see her, Dad?'

I tried to remain vague, airy. 'She's often over on business. I expect I'll see her again soon.'

His sister, Alice, who is never slow to catch on, joined in the act. 'Do you still love her, Dad?'

Hey! I thought. What is this? The Spanish Inquisition? Are these monsters my kids? I tried, as I always do, to take refuge in irony, but I could not shake them off.

'I liked Ruth,' said Charlie. 'She used to give terrific presents.'

Alice was grimly smothering her french fries with ketch-up. 'She once gave me a toy koala, but I didn't like it when she tried to kiss me goodnight.'

'Granma says Ruth wears too much lipstick,' said Charlie.

Now they were in full cry, heartlessly dissecting their recollections of my great affair. After a while I interrupted their fun to explain that Ruth and I were just friends now. Besides, I said, she was planning to leave London and go home to Australia.

20

Alice looked up from her plate. 'What exactly is the point of Australia?'

Precocious brat. Sometimes I hate our schoolkids. Give me English slow-starters any day.

Alice was persisting. 'I mean, why does Ruth want to go to Australia?'

'Because –' Actually, I had no idea. 'Because her family lives there,' I said. 'She likes the sun,' I added, hoping to find the safety of neutral ground.

'Can we go to Australia?' Alice, commuting between her parents, has become an enthusiastic flyer. Sometimes I see her, grown-up, jetting around the world with a credit card and a lightweight suitcase, troubleshooting for some corporation. She knows no fear and has her mother's self-possession.

The conversation lost momentum, and then meandered into vacations and schools. Ruth faded as suddenly as she had appeared.

I have to admit their curiosity is natural. I myself have to confront more than her memory. Ruth has always had something of a knack for timing, good or bad depending on your point of view, and by one of those coincidences she has always revelled in she will be here the day after tomorrow. Thankfully, the kids will have gone home. Heaven knows what Lizzie would have said if they'd all met.

Ruth is in Boston. As usual, she is doing three things at once and not telling anyone exactly what. When pressed she admitted she had a local TV station to meet with, and then two days free. The visit was her idea. A postcard of a rock ape from Gibraltar and then a call, late at night. I must confess I was astonished. It's been nearly two years since we were last together, and when we parted on that occasion it seemed obvious that we should not see each other again. When she telephoned I resisted, but not for long.

I have a photograph of Ruth as she was in those days buried among a collage of snapshots on the bulletin board in

21

the kitchen. We were in Spain, tracing the pilgrim's route to Santiago de Compostela, staying in parador hotels like any couple. Ruth, quickly tiring of the churches, announced she was dying for a swim. I was anxious to please her, so we made a detour north to the coast. This is not the Costa del Sol. You could be in Maine or Scotland. There's heather on the clifftops and the Atlantic thunders onto deserted beaches. Ruth took her clothes off and bobbed about in the freezing surf. I watched, sitting above the tide among the dunes.

When she came shivering out of the waves she insisted I take her photograph. She is proud of her body. She faced up to the camera naked, head thrown back in laughter, arms stretched up in sun worship. I threw her a towel. She rubbed herself dry and then we made love. Afterwards I snapped her again, still flushed and breathless, in close-up. The picture was intended to be a private joke, an erotic souvenir, for the two of us. Yet, as it happens, this was our last holiday together, in retrospect a doomed attempt to make things work. By then, I'm sad to say, too much had gone wrong between us. You would never have guessed that within minutes of my taking that photo she would be sobbing like a child. And I never guessed – or did I? – what it was that would destroy her composure. As Marshall observed on more than one occasion, Who says the camera never lies?

I don't miss her, not now, but, together with Marshall she has exercised a special grip on my life that only my father's death could release. In this respect I'm more than a trifle curious about her forthcoming visit.

6

Now the children have gone back and I'm alone again, trying to make sense of things past. You could say they only make sense today, June 15th, 1982, but that's too simple. I have been closing in, my quarry in the cross-hairs, ever since my father's funeral. Ruth's imminent arrival only serves to bring a moving target into focus and perhaps to remind me of the disastrous experiment in English life I have put behind me.

The Old Country is very much in the news at the moment. As I was getting up this morning, there was some jocular banter on the television about 'the empire on which the sun never sets', one of those silly, apparently unscripted, exchanges between the anchor woman and the weatherman, a young black for whom 'the empire' must be as remote and meaningless as the Stone Age.

I found myself irritated and offended by their flippancy. My whole life has seen the decline of that 'empire'. I was eleven when British troops landed at Suez and fifteen when Kennedy was elected. I grew up, over here, watching and protesting at the failure of another imperial adventure in South-East Asia. It's been a bad time for superpowers, but a good time for nationalism. I look at the Union Jack on the TV screen and wonder what the future will hold.

I've been intrigued to wonder how we would have managed these recent events. We never had to fight a hot war. When I say 'we', I mean the President and his staff. At least to start with, we were rather collegiate. We prided ourselves on voicing our opinions to each other and being heard. There were times when the White House resembled a graduate seminar, not a seat of government.

What line would we have taken? The President, an engineer and a Christian, thought no problem couldn't be solved by reason and goodness. I would have helped draft a speech about the morality of international relations, the illegality of force, the importance of national sovereignty and perhaps the right of self-determination.

We were still sore from Vietnam then, and saw each overseas emergency as a potential quagmire to be avoided at all cost. Of course, we had to exercise some international muscle, so we fixed on 'human rights' in a variety of two-bit Third World dictatorships. This was shadow boxing, but we persuaded ourselves that we were still in the ring. I like to think we would have stopped the recent drama long before the shooting started, but who knows?

The British will certainly take the credit for their victory, but there's no doubt that it was 'the cousins' who made it possible. This is how the cookie crumbles. No wonder some Brits still idolise the United States. That's a two-way street, in my experience. Despite my best efforts, even my children are not immune to some romanticism about their grandfather and his peculiar ways. As Mother has often said, 'The English are a funny people.' On both sides of the Atlantic there are so many misconceptions about the farther shore.

Last night, the children and I were heading off for a farewell dinner down on the waterfront when Alice said: 'Can I have lobster, Dad?'

Alice is fascinated by lobsters. To her, they're a kind of exotic natural toy. 'Sure,' I said, ever the indulgent father.

'When we stayed with Granpa,' said Charlie, 'he used to let us put the lobsters in the boiling water.' He made a long face and mimicked an Oxford accent. 'It's the old, classical question, my dear Charles. "Does the crustacean feel pain?" '

Alice said: 'Of course they feel pain. You can hear them squeak.'

A few minutes later, I watched the thrill in her eyes as she pressed her face to the tank and passed sentence. When the waiter brought her shell-pink victim to our table, I saw in her parted lips the glamour of execution.

I was restless. I look forward to their visits, especially in these summer months, but it's always too brief and hectic. We're just beginning to get to know each other again when it's time to head off for the plane that will take them home to their mother. Now there's only the debris, scattered videos and an unfinished game of Monopoly, to remind me of their invasion. A red circle around Ruth's name on my day-planner advertises the next engagement.

Military jargon is in the air at the moment. On 'Good Morning America' today it was 'unconditional surrender'. A diplomat with wounded eyes and a Spanish lisp was gamely asserting his people's right to those islands, but when you see the Union Jack fluttering over the tin rooftops, and the columns of defeated prisoners, you realise that this is the arrogance of despair.

I know the feeling. We all have our pride. I was never more assertive than when I was inwardly lost. Alone here with my memories I can hang out the white flag and sue for peace with the warring forces within. Admitting the truth about yourself can be an exhilarating experience, like declaring bankruptcy. I am enjoying the gamble of uncharted territory. Who knows what will happen next?

I remember the Old Man, who liked to show off his education, quoting Napoleon: 'On s'engage et puis on voit.' One day we had visitors from the State Department. A smart-ass lawyer, who didn't give a damn, asked what he meant.

'Well,' said my boss, lengthening the vowel in the Southern fashion, 'w-e-ll, it kind of means, "Let's do it." ' He flashed that famous, toothy, nervy smile of his. 'Right, Mister Gilchrist?'

I liked it when he addressed me in that kidding way. Nerdish as it may sound, I liked to have my European savoir-faire recognised. In a world in which everyone was casually Bob and Gene and Chuck, it made me feel part of some nebulous inner circle. This was an illusion, of course. Too rarely would I get to play on the White House tennis court. A seductive illusion, nonetheless. I'm afraid it was quite satisfying to be able to remark, in conversation, what the President had said the night before.

I have tried to put DC behind me, but Mother calls from Washington two or three times a week. When she has finished ranting about the present Administration, gossiped about the goings-on inside the Beltway, and moaned about the disgraceful decline in public life, she often turns to my father's memory, generally in the context of her hopes that I will not follow in his footsteps. She will joke about her 'wicked husband', but it's a thrust that opens something inside both of us like an incurable wound, and I always try to change the subject.

It's a losing battle. Apart from Lizzie, my ex, and the kids, I'm all she's got. She's always had too much riding on me. After the wedding and two stolen nights by Lake Windermere, he went back to his destroyer at Scapa Flow and she went south again to take dictation from Eisenhower. But my heart was beating in her womb and later, when she discovered she could have no more, that single experience of motherhood became unbearably precious. She was still in khaki when I was born, but the fighting was virtually over.

My own children, Charlie especially, are fascinated by that war. They learn it as we learned about the Greeks and Romans. How far off and strange it seems when they ask about Hitler or Churchill and the sinking of the *Bismarck*. I look at the television. This latest adventure seems ludicrous by comparison. My parents' war was about something, a real defence of vital freedoms. But this? Borges is right. Here we have the spectacle of two bald men fighting over a comb.

Mother rang yesterday to speak to the children. 'It's Granma,' I said. Charlie made a face. He's that age. Alice takes after Lizzie: she gives good phone, yakking away while the men of the household stand by. I watch my son watching his sister and wonder what he is thinking. Sometimes I get a shiver up my spine when I see how much he loves her. And then, a moment later, I will have to stop them squabbling over a pop video, and Alice's funny round face will be flushed with tears and rage.

Finally, it's my turn. For a moment we speculate about the end of hostilities. Mother is predictably scornful of the Brits. Apparently they – should I say 'we'? – have had all kinds of clandestine assistance from Washington. 'Perhaps,' she says, 'there is a Special Relationship after all.'

'That's one way to describe it,' I chip in, with a telephone laugh. I don't really know what else to say. Once, when I had my finger on the pulse, I would have bounced back with some in-house gossip of my own. Now, in my frayed shirt and beach shorts, I feel ill-informed and out of touch.

In the silence she starts in on me. Was I looking after the children? Was Alice taking her medicine? Why was I still on the Cape? I should hurry up and get the script done. I was too young to drop out. Hollywood was a mistake, all her friends said so. It was not serious. I should come back to DC and get a real job. She'd heard on the grapevine that so-and-so . . . I held up my end as well as I could. Charlie came over while she was in full flood. I raised my eyebrows and a look of joyous fraternity passed between us.

I'm glad to say I relate pretty well to my son, and vice versa. Psychologically speaking, I suppose that's predictable. When it comes to fatherhood, I am anxious not to repeat the mistakes of the previous generation.

7

I might have guessed that Ruth's visit to the Cape would revive the worst of the past. My father's death is only half the story. True to her old form, it was Ruth who brought me face to face with Marshall's fate once more. This time I had no excuse. I was already committed to getting to grips with some difficult stuff. After she left, I would have no choice but to pull out my dusty White House diaries and dig deeper into the interstices of memory.

In anticipation, naturally, I had been anxious. I was up early, making the house ready, and clearing away the empties in the kitchen. Ruth has a sharp eye for evidence of my weakness. It was barely nine o'clock when I cooked myself a condemned man's breakfast, in fortification for the day ahead.

I sat on the deck, savouring the scent of privet blossom, and let the breath of the morning, the distant thunder of the ocean, calm my spirits. Then, abandoning my routine, I headed off into town for some last-minute luxuries. I wanted to convince myself that today was a vacation.

The town is as pretty as a picture in the sunshine. The light dazzles from the clapboard, the sidewalk is warm as a new loaf, and the boats bobbing at anchor seem to be part of the summer's dance. It's at moments like this that I know I can never live in England again. In his unguarded, Anglophile moments, Herb will speak of the 'barbarism' of American life, but he is talking about the cities. Once you escape, as I've done, to the dreaming seashore, there's nowhere on earth to match it.

I like to think that in some unconscious way this is to do with the memory of our forefathers. Occasionally, when

I'm in the mood, I drive to the point where, it is said, they first came ashore. I try to picture the scene, the cold and the wet, the exhausted travellers' relief, but I can summon no detail that will bring the moment to life for me. There are some stories of adventure and self-sacrifice that will always defy our powers of analysis and recall.

On this day, then, I completed my shopping on Bradford Street, collected the mail, scanned the headlines in the *Globe* and then, sooner than I had intended, drove the ten minutes to the local airport, a landing strip popular with light commuter planes in summer.

Arrivals and departures pass through the same nondescript building. In the winter, waiting for a connection to Boston, I have been almost alone here but today there was a family crowd. I recognised one of my neighbours, a heavy-looking banker in a pinstripe suit, as awkward as a mortician in a toy store. He was telling anyone who would listen about his visits to what he called 'Blighty', but I suspect that he was less familiar with the Old World than he wanted us to believe.

Ruth's flight was on time. I strolled outside and watched the elderly turboprop touch down with a bounce and a puff of tyre-rubber, brake, turn and taxi across the apron with a roar. The rotor blades were still spinning when Ruth, first off and fresh as a daisy, stepped onto the tarmac.

'Darling.' She held out her arms to me and, after a momentary hesitation, I lifted her up, as I would in the old days. She was as light as I remembered, lithe and firm. We kissed. I think we were both relieved to find so much warmth and excitement between us.

I collected her bag, she took my arm and we walked over to the car. If you had been watching us, standing among the friends and relatives at the gate, you would have supposed we were man and wife.

I opened the passenger door and then we embraced again, sizing each other up. Ruth seemed as trim as ever, stylish but

29

not overdressed. Her china-blue eyes checked me out, as they always had, with the searching penetration of a camera.

We drove along the ocean road to the house. Ruth was bubbling over with excitement and approval. I had barely parked the car before she was insisting we go for a swim.

Before I knew it we were scuffing across the dunes to the beach. Then she was skipping into the shallows and fighting through the surf. She broke into an energetic crawl. Just to watch her made me feel out of shape, but I joined her anyway, though we did not cling and kiss as we might have done in the past.

Then we stretched out on the sand and caught up with each other's lives. I told her about my recent crisis, wanting her to know how far I'd fallen. She confessed she'd been through a bad time, too. I said I thought things were starting to look up. She said she hoped to go back to Australia. I said that I, too, was cutting my connection with England, and she said how sorry she was to read about my father. She had been in Hong Kong at the time. If she had been in Europe she would have made a point of coming to the funeral.

I said nothing.

Secretly, I was glad she had been in the Far East. I would not have wanted her at the funeral. Indeed, it had been my fear that she would turn up anyway.

'How's your love life?'

I'd forgotten how direct she was. 'I don't have one.' I poked evasively at the beach with a bit of driftwood. 'And you?'

She laughed in that merry way I remembered and launched into a slightly scandalous story about a lawyer ('married, of course') whom she'd seduced at a wedding in Berlin. 'So you see,' she concluded, apparently without a trace of self-consciousness, 'I'm still up to my old tricks.'

I traced a pattern in the sand. 'Am I one of your old tricks?'

Ruth looked at me. I saw the warning light in her eyes. 'Come on, Sam. Don't be a dag.'

She turned away and looked out to sea, as if censoring herself in my presence. I waited, expecting more, but she stayed silent and our thoughts were interrupted by a gang of children chasing through the waves.

Ruth came out of her reverie. 'How are the kids?'

'Terrifying.' I explained how grown-up they were getting.

Ruth laughed. 'Before you know it, Charlie will be bringing girls home for the night.'

'If he takes after his grandfather,' I said.

She smiled, and changed the subject. 'How was the funeral? Was it awful?'

'Actually, no. It was fine.' I did not choose to elaborate. I wanted her to understand where the limits were. I began to describe my new mood of self-criticism.

During my sojourn on the Cape I had decided, I told her, that I should face up to myself. When you're young, you're interested in the externals, what we call 'the real world'. As you get older you become more interested in yourself, aware of time and infirmity, and that's scary.

'Especially for youth-conscious high-flyers,' she said with a teasing laugh.

'I don't feel like a high-flyer,' I said, 'and I'm approaching forty. Shakespeare was writing *Hamlet* when he was my age.'

'Excuse me, darling, but hacking out a screenplay for Herb Schulz is not exactly the same as writing an Elizabethan tragic masterpiece.' Ruth knew how to prick my fantasy bubble. 'I mean – Sam –' She waved at the beach. 'This is about as "responsible" as – as a day at the beach.'

'You haven't seen what else I'm writing.'

'Will you show me?'

'If you're good.'

'I wonder what that means.'

We climbed back up the beach towards the house. When we reached my land, Ruth stopped me at the gate. 'A kissing gate,' she said, putting out her arms.

I shook my head, then thought better of it, and kissed her quickly on the cheek.

She held me by the arm, and her wide eyes zoomed in. 'Forgiven?' she said.

I looked away across the sand. 'Forgiven.'

We strolled across the grass, arm in arm. She pointed at the flagpole. 'You should fly the flag.'

I smiled. Ruth loves to organise people's lives, especially mine.

She recognised my expression. 'I know, I know – I can't help it.'

Memories of the old days returned. I said nothing, but squeezed her arm, and stared down, watching my bare feet pace across the prickly grass.

'Something on your mind?'

We had reached the deck. I paused on the step and looked into her eyes. 'You,' I said.

She protested.

'In a manner of speaking,' I added, back-tracking quickly.

I think she knew what I meant because she gave an uneasy laugh and ran inside, saying that she would take a shower.

I went over to my desk and played my messages. Herb. Mother. Herb again. The kids. Nothing that couldn't wait. We had dawdled on the beach. I was surprised to see that it was nearly three o'clock. The sun was high, the sky brilliant. Across the hall I could hear Ruth singing in the shower. I hesitated, fiddling idly with the top button of my shirt. Then I went into the kitchen and fixed some drinks, a summer cocktail of my own devising, one part gin and one part vodka to three parts Seven-Up, with a dash of angostura bitters.

As I was crushing the ice, Ruth came through, barefoot, in a shapeless white caftan. Her hair hung damply in dark snakes on her neck and I knew she was naked under her robe. She was holding an envelope in her right hand. This was a moment I had anticipated and feared, and it killed the moment of desire stone-dead.

I saw my name in Marshall's familiar handwriting, and took the letter. I wanted to tear it open at once, and at the same time I wanted never to read it.

'Go on,' said Ruth.

I hesitated still. There would be nothing new in what he had to say.

'I'll look at it later.'

'He's not just sending his condolences,' she replied.

Marshall's handwriting was always crammed between the lines of his prison notepaper, and his words were violently scored onto the page. I glanced at the first paragraph. The familiar appeal. The tangle of apology, reproach and accusation. If he had been with me, I might have put a hand on his shoulder, might have said: 'It's okay, Craig. You can rest now. I have begun. At last the world can judge.' Instead, I looked at Ruth. 'Whose idea was this?'

'Mine.' She shrugged. 'The man's in jail, Sam.'

'That's what I'm writing,' I said, hoping to deflate her. 'His story. Your story.' I went over to my desk and picked up my notebook. 'My story. Here,' I said. 'You always could read my writing.'

She studied the page for a moment. 'In at the deep end,' she quoted. 'You're five years too late, Sam.'

'Better late than never.'

'He's still inside.'

'You know you can't blame me for that.'

'I will if you let him down again.' She faced me. I sensed she was giving me one more chance. 'You have no excuse now,' she said.

As I come to this moment now, I see she was right. Even then, as she spoke, I realised I no longer felt defensive, or protective. Perhaps for the first time, I was ready to confront the past as I knew it. As Shakespeare says, the lines are in front of me as I write, 'There is a history in all men's lives, fighting the nature of the times deceased.'

33

1979

1

How could I ever forget the Christmas of Seventy-Nine? The liberation of a new start! I was going back to the drawing-board, back to the future. I believed I was in free fall, but strictly speaking I had a parachute. However much I might like to, I cannot shake off my childhood. England will always be my second home, and inevitably there was my father, watching from the wings.

The habits of control die hard. He was on the phone with his habitual greeting almost the minute I arrived. 'It's the Beaver speaking.' He wanted to know, as he put it, what the hell was going on. I might have been a wayward junior. If he could have seen my hotel bedroom, with Ruth and the Sunday papers sprawled beside me, he would have understood at a glance. I said I would explain and, counter-attacking, asked how he was: 'I look all right,' he replied, 'but I feel bloody awful.' He was having treatment in the hospital. Jane was being 'a perfect angel'. I was glad. I did not want that responsibility. When he asked after Mother, I hurried the conversation forward. I would call him when I had found my feet. I was planning, I said, still unconsciously American, to take a short-term lease somewhere 'downtown'.

When I rang a week later and told him I was settled in St John's Wood, he teased my idea of 'downtown', made some crack about Arabs and call-girls, and abused me, quite amiably, for giving up a good job in Washington. His real concern was for my family, especially his grandchildren. 'What's going on with you and Lizzie?' I told him we were having a trial separation. 'Trial balls,' he replied. 'You're with that girl of yours. I wasn't born yesterday.' I confessed I was in love with Ruth and feared that my

37

marriage was over. When it came to emotional matters, he was always practical. 'I'm sure you know what you're up to,' were his parting words. 'Just let me know when you want me to meet her.'

Actually, I had no idea what I was up to. I was improvising, going on instinct. I knew I was on a treadmill at home and at work. When Ruth first came into my life I had resisted the invitation to escape. For two years I had lived adulterously and had grown hollow with the lie. Finally, I told myself I had no choice. 'Come on,' she said. 'Trust yourself for a change.' It was an opportunity I had to seize. Ruth would not stay in London forever. 'Why not?' I replied. My next call was to Pan Am, and before I knew it I was booked. 'How will you pay for that, sir?' I hesitated, then gave my credit card. 'May I have your billing address, please sir?' As I repeated street and zip code it was as though I was giving my home away to a stranger, releasing myself from my troubles.

There was, in this move, more than an element of professional calculation. By Thanksgiving that year, the White House had become, as Herb liked to say, 'as much fun as a mortuary on Yom Kippur'. The President was the prisoner of the Rose Garden, wrapping himself in the Stars and Stripes for comfort.

Remember Iran? When the crisis broke many people had barely heard of the place. Only a few could, with confidence, locate it on a map. I remember the first time someone referred to Islamic fundamentalism in a meeting. What the hell is an 'ayatollah', we all wondered. The more we discovered about Khomeini, the more appalled we became. How could we do business with such a vengeful monster?

It was so unfair. In the honeymoon days, after the triumphant inauguration, we were just working hard to be nice to people, playing world community cop, not international John Wayne. This suited the President. He was a decent guy trying to do his best by his country and worrying himself to death with just about everything under the sun. He was less like a President than any President I've ever seen, more his own Chief of Staff. He liked to call his job 'one big multiple-choice exam', and surrounded himself with policy nerds as though he was cramming for Finals.

In those days, Washington resembled a gambling town that had suddenly got religion. People were talking about 'the American dream' again. The President had his promises compiled into a book and issued to the press. 'I will not lie to you,' he assured us, and, amazingly enough, we did not laugh in his face.

When the hostages were seized, the dream, such as it was, came to an end, and the nightmare began. We were the Great Satan. Suddenly there were fifty-two Americans in the hands of this bunch of crazies with dish-cloths on their heads, toting Soviet automatic weapons, and screaming Death to US Imperialists! We were powerless. The shame. The frustration. The anger. Americans are bad losers, and worst of all, the President did not know what to do.

I thought I knew what to do, and that was save my own skin. I resigned. At the time, I thought I was taking control of my life, but actually I was about to take a dive. So, in retrospect, I had something in common with my boss. Towards the end of his term, it was as though he was jinxed, with one piece of bad luck after another. Even when he went jogging for charity that fall, he'd stumbled, exhausted, watched by the world's media. He seemed, at that moment, literally done for.

The day before I quit, the Old Man called me into the Oval Office. It was typical of him that he should want to say goodbye. We chatted about the hostage crisis. Khomeini was threatening to put the 'American spies' on trial. No one seemed to know what was happening in Tehran. After a minute or two, he thanked me for what I had done. He seemed tired and grey. There was a child's model of a Thanksgiving turkey on his desk, a present from his daughter. He made a joke at his own expense, but there was no laughter in his eyes. As I got up to go, he said: 'Well, Sam, how did I do?'

I looked at him with astonishment. He sincerely wanted to know. He wanted his term paper marked. For a moment I couldn't think how to reply, then I found the metaphor. 'You took the game to the other side,' I said.

He seemed pleased. 'I used to play in college. I wanted to be a quarterback, but . . .' We shook hands, with the sentence hanging in the air between us, and then I walked out of the White House for ever. If, unconsciously, I thought such a move would release me from Marshall's peculiar obsession with my special role in his unfortunate life I could not have been more mistaken.

2

My new address, as my father had suggested, was in a neighbourhood associated with fast, expensive women and Middle Eastern businessmen, a short walk from the Abbey Road of Beatles fame. My landlord, Mr Upjohn, might have stepped straight from the Sixties himself. With his long sideburns, wide lapels and aggressively demotic accent, he could have been an extra from *A Hard Day's Night*. His long nose and lugubrious Habsburg jaw gave his speech the tone of an underwater foghorn. 'I think you will find,' he boomed, putting the key in the lock, 'that this is a very nice maisonette.'

It was not. The front door opened onto a dark passageway. The 'spacious lounge' was a pair of mean-looking rooms separated by a battered pine partition. At the back, the eat-in kitchen looked onto an overgrown garden weirdly populated with a family of plastic gnomes. There was a draught from the side door and Mr Upjohn, turning to escort me upstairs, trumpeted something about 'fixing the french windows in this regard'. At the top of the stairs, there were two gloomy bedrooms and an avocado-green bathroom without a shower. 'What we have here,' said Mr Upjohn, his voice booming in the confined space, 'is vacant possession for immediate residency.' He seemed tacitly to admit that it had no other recommendation.

'I'll take it,' I said. I did not want to be homeless for Christmas, and it was a roof I could afford.

Mr Upjohn looked startled, as if cornered by a loan shark. When he began to intone the terms and conditions, I hurried him back to his office, rang my bank and my lawyer, and paid three months down. 'Where I come from,' I said, 'we expect same-day service.'

Ruth's reaction was predictable. She stopped by the next afternoon, on her way to a conference in Bonn. 'At least it has a phone.' She was relieved, I now see, that I had not insisted on moving into her place. 'I'll call you tonight.'

I watched her write the address and telephone number in her book and thought: This is where I begin again.

Ruth had a taxi waiting outside. I waved goodbye and then, buttoning my coat, set off to explore my new habitat.

When the curtain goes up on my memories of that time, I am walking down the street towards the Finchley Road. I have just bought an electric kettle, four mugs, and half a pound of Earl Grey. I'm curiously elated. The sky's the limit. The world is my oyster. I am in love. I am free. The map of my life seems new. Only my wife's letters from across the Atlantic, the accusing face of Thomas Jefferson staring from the top right-hand corner, could remind me of what I had left behind.

I say 'curiously' because if I'd stopped to analyse my position, I might have felt isolated and uncertain. I might even have felt a trifle reckless. But that was the point. I wanted to live dangerously. I wanted the sensation of getting in touch with my own life.

For three years I had lived vicariously, in the service of someone else, my very words subordinate to his authority. Pouring yourself into someone else's life is morally draining. There was some job satisfaction, but not much recognition. Of all the many things demanded of him, there was nothing the President disliked more than giving speeches. If my words went well, I was invisible. If they went badly, I caught the flak. Even though the Old Man was (as the newspapers like to put it) the most powerful person on earth, I was just a tiny figure in the crowded antechamber of greatness.

I remember when we were working on the first fireside chat. The President called two or three of us into his office and gave us a good-natured lecture, 'for future reference'.

He was sitting at his desk, with classical music, some kind of baroque symphony, playing in the background. He had our draft in his hand. We should avoid, he said, using abstract words such as 'cynical'. The average person wouldn't understand them.

'Whenever I make a speech,' he said, 'I think of a simple fellow I know who has a gas station down in Lumpkin, Georgia. If I was talking to him, I'd say "callous" not "cynical". Working people understand callouses. See, their hands get hard.'

We admired his instincts, I guess, but his calculated simplicity was in danger of boring his political staff to death. The White House lost its charisma and became a boondoggle for ambitious young careerists. No one much enjoyed what they were doing, but even the greyest grad school dweebs knew it would look good on their résumés. The guys who had the fun were the hacks down the hall, the political fixers who did the deals with the Hill, but they were high on their own excitement, and kept themselves apart. There was no room here for the passionate or the unconventional. You learned conformity. You learned not to make waves. If you wanted to hint at personality, you went Anglophile, shopped in Knightsbridge and flashed your English labels.

I took Ruth to Harrods that week before Christmas. I wanted to buy her something showy and expensive, and also to get presents for the children. My colleague, Herb Schulz, was flying back to Washington from some overseas junket and had offered to act as courier. By chance, moving in the festive crush from the perfume counter to the toy department, we found ourselves in the pet shop.

Alice, who was just eight then, had agitated all summer for a marmalade cat, and finally Lizzie and I had promised her one for Christmas. Now the time had come and I was alone, looking at puppies and kittens and guinea-pigs. I remembered the happiness in Alice's face as she rushed about the house repeating 'pussycat, pussycat', and my eyes filled with tears.

I had sung to her at bedtime. 'Pussycat, pussycat, where have you been? I've been up to London to visit the Queen.'

Ruth, who had been admiring a cage of humming-birds, saw that I was wistful. 'Come on,' she said. 'Let's go and play.'

'Play' was her word. With me, she was always playing. I have never known a woman of the world who feared seriousness in a relationship as she did.

In those early days we would go to late-night movies or have dim sum at one o'clock in the morning. We would get up late and read five newspapers before having brunch in Soho. We had never been alone together for more than a weekend, and our rendezvous had always been clandestine. Now it was a pleasure to walk into a restaurant or a theatre foyer and not have to worry about the gossips who might catch us holding hands.

I could never pin her down absolutely. She would change countries the way some women change clothes. There was always the possibility of that pip-pip call from the pay phone. 'Darling, I'm at Heathrow. I have to go to Amsterdam. See you tomorrow. Ciao.'

At first, I tried to inquire what, exactly, was taking her away. I soon discovered this was a mistake. She did not like to be questioned. She would become cold and distant and irritable. 'I'm a journo,' she would say. 'I have stories to cover.' She was writing for the Australian press, so I rarely, if ever, saw her copy or by-line. I had to take her on trust. Looking back, I see that she enjoyed making this demand.

Of course, she more than compensated for her sudden absences. When she was with me, she took over completely. Everything about her was so vivid. Her clothes, I remember, were the colours of the rainbow. She had the figure for tight, provocative dresses, and she knew it. She would alter the tint of her hair on a whim, from blonde to brunette in an afternoon. She would wear secretary-bird glasses one day,

44

shades the next, and contact lenses the third. Her apartment was like a theatrical dressing-room. One week she would buy scented Moroccan candles, another week she would be experimenting with massage oil. I don't mean to suggest that she was kinky, just that she liked to express herself through her body. The French have a phrase for it, *'bien dans sa peau'*.

When I think of that time now, I suppose I should remember her laughter and her love of fun, but memory is not always a loyal friend. Once the first flush of adventure had passed, I regret to admit that my life became once again crowded with a host of anxieties. I worried about my children, I worried about Lizzie, I worried about myself and, as I'll explain shortly, I found myself worrying about Marshall too.

My plan was to set up a PR consultancy, acting as a go-between for British and American companies. I had even settled on a name for the business that was, I thought, at once apt, witty and ironic: The Special Relationship.

I leased a couple of rooms in Covent Garden, applied for a telephone, advertised for an assistant and commissioned some office stationery. I'd already gotten promises of work from friends and contacts in Washington and Whitehall. I told myself that my father's old-school-tie network would come in handy. When I was not goofing off with Ruth, I would get up early, put on my suit and head into town to pitch to prospective clients. I believed my political credentials would stand me in good stead. Everyone agreed that I should not have too much difficulty in getting the business off the ground. Brits, I assumed, would be impressed by American media savvy.

I discovered I could have it both ways. To prospective British clients I played the street-wise American. To my fellow countrymen, I was more pukka than the duke. I had no difficulty with either part and I found that, psychologically speaking, people preferred to trust what they recognised but did not know.

In all these meetings there was, of course, no reckoning. My balance-sheet was clean. The only faint drumbeat of doubt came from my inner knowledge that I would never have taken me on. Perhaps my versatility was my undoing. Who knows? It was only later that I discovered the perfidious nature of an English promise.

Then, almost out of the blue, I was called to account, but not in the way I expected. You could say my personal audit began on the day my car conked out.

3

One of my first moves, on arriving in London, had been to get myself some wheels from a used-car salesman in Kilburn. After the usual horse-trading, we struck a deal and I found myself in possession of a mustard-yellow VW Beetle. At first, it was strange to be driving on the left, and stranger still, after my spacious gas-guzzler, to be crammed in the front like a Gemini astronaut. Soon, I appreciated its nifty way with metropolitan traffic, and even down the highway, on those occasions when Ruth and I took off into the country, it motored happily from A to B.

On this morning, however, the car would not start. The battery was dead, kaputski. I had an appointment with a potential client in town and I was anxious not to be late. In some agitation, I hurried to the Maida Vale Tube, snatched a newspaper from the stand, and found a seat in the last car. I skimmed the headlines, glanced at the sports section, and then began to browse. The train pulled into Warwick Road. A crowd of schoolkids, laughing and chattering, surged on board, then the doors closed with a rumble and we rattled deeper into the sooty darkness. The lights flickered, went out, and came on again. I was casually scanning the Home News when I saw the item: Inquest Adjourned.

'The inquest into the death of Jeffrey Roberts, the Bournemouth bookseller, was adjourned to the New Year following the presentation of new evidence by the police. The coroner . . .'

Now the truth is that I was feeling bad about this story. I had been so caught up with my own problems that I had pushed it to the back of my mind. Roberts, of course, was quite unknown to me, though his death had made the news in a small way. He had been involved with a popular television programme and had died in mysterious circumstances. No, my dilemma was simple. The chief witness in the case was a certain Craig Bathurst Marshall, formerly a major with Her Majesty's armed services.

When Ruth had first mentioned the matter soon after my arrival in London I was surprised, even intrigued, but in the rush and whirl of those first weeks my curiosity was a strictly limited commodity. I suppose I told myself I would catch up with Marshall's latest problems in due course. I'd every reason to be wary.

Now I was running out of excuses. I could not act dumb: here was the cold print of a national newspaper. I could no longer play the globe-trotting American: I was living in London. I spent the rest of my journey wondering what to do. Ruth was out of town. I could not speak to her until that evening. Should I attempt to track down Marshall's phone number? The day passed in stop-go prevarication. I bought the evening paper in the hope of further news, but the story had dropped out of sight.

I was at home, preparing a TV dinner, when Ruth called. I tried to explain my difficulty, but she was dismissive. Sure, I was feeling guilty. 'You let him down,' she said.

I ignored this. 'You must have his number,' I said. 'Shall I phone him?'

'I'll phone him.' There was a coldness in her voice that said she was weary of my indecisiveness, and I confess I now regret seeming such a wimp.

We agreed, before she rang off, that she would come back to me with Marshall's response, but I waited in vain. It was nearly eleven o'clock when my patience ran out and I called her hotel. The receptionist answered in broken English that 'Miss Rich' had gone out with 'some men'. No, he had no idea when she would be back. I fell asleep, slightly drunk, and woke the next morning feeling terrible. My car was still not fixed, I had another breakfast meeting and I was late again. Worst of all, I had no news about Marshall.

But when I came home that evening I had a surprise in store.

It was dark as I turned the corner into my street. When there were no airplanes overhead it was quiet, almost provincial. Suddenly, I had this sensation that I was being watched. I hurried past the line of parked cars, past my neighbours' illuminated Christmas trees, then paused to catch my breath and take stock. A buzzing yellow street-light cast my shadow against the front door, but that was all. I have to admit that my hand was shaking as I put the key in the lock.

Inside, the house was quiet. I stood in the hall for a moment, listening to the refrigerator's purr and the creak of the central heating. Then I switched on the lights and went upstairs.

Suddenly, I was racing.

Nothing in the bathroom, the dishevelled bedroom just as it was, downstairs again, the living-room cheerless but undisturbed, the kitchen cold and uninviting.

Now I felt calmer. Next door, someone was practising scales on a piano. I opened the freezer to consider my evening menu.

At that moment, the doorbell rang.

I stood still and waited. The bell rang again, apparently louder and more insistent. I walked towards the front door. The bell rang a third time. I put my hand to the latch, then hesitated. 'Who is it?' My words sounded tinny in my ears.

'Is that you, Seymour?'

This was the voice, the challenge of the Scottish elder, I had been dreading.

I opened the door. Marshall was on the doorstep, more than ever the B-movie actor in a trench-coat and tweed cap. He was much as I remembered him, though smaller perhaps, and less ebullient than before.

'Come in,' I said, meeting his firm, military handshake.

He crossed the threshold like a debt-collector, throwing

his coat and cap over the banister. As I showed him into the living-room and offered him a drink I noticed how well turned out he always seemed to be. The pride Marshall took in his appearance made his humiliation in the world seem all the more painful.

'I read about you in the paper,' I said, handing him a large scotch.

'Ruth said.' Her name came between us, a warning shot. 'Cheers.'

'Cheers.' I raised my glass with a bonhomie I did not feel.

'She said you wanted to see me,' he added. His watchful smile was like a mask. 'So here I am.'

It was, of course, not true that I wanted to see him. How could I begin to explain? The Seymour J. Gilchrist he had met three summers ago was no longer sitting before him. Then, I was hungry for a story that seemed to offer a necessary explanation. Now, I was trying to escape that web.

'I quit my job,' I said.

'Then we have something in common,' he replied.

'My Dad is probably dying. I'm no longer the man for you.' I wanted to keep this interview short and sweet and send him on his way with the minimum of fuss. If I thought I could throw him off that easily, I was mistaken.

'Seymour,' he said, playing the oldest line in the script like a trooper, 'I'm in deep shit. You can't let me down this time.'

On another occasion I might have smiled at his language. Now I just shook my head with dismay and tried to explain that, in a manner of speaking, I had already done just that. He said nothing, but his expression was full of reproach. I repeated that I felt an obligation to my father.

I felt his Labrador eyes study me as I spoke. When I finished he said simply: 'But you made me a promise.' In the world in which Marshall had grown up a promise was a bond of loyalty not lightly set aside.

50

'I know, I know.' I felt so tired. Here was a responsibility I did not want right now. I attempted to find a note of jocularity and move the conversation on a tad. 'I gather you've added a few chapters to your story.'

'I'll say,' he replied. 'It is, of course, nothing that I could not have predicted.'

'Don't be ridiculous,' I said.

I could see he was hurt, and I'm afraid I was glad. I wanted him to understand I was no longer the bright-eyed, bushy-tailed youngster of our first meeting.

'Okay, Seymour,' he admitted, 'I'm exaggerating. But not much.'

I smiled. 'I'll say one thing for you, Major. You always seem to have a tale to tell.'

In his intuitive way, he knew what I was thinking. 'You don't believe me, do you?'

I shook my head involuntarily. 'No,' I replied. 'I don't suppose I do.'

'I know you'll always give me a fair hearing, Seymour.' When he wanted, he knew how to turn on the charm. 'Then you can decide.'

'OK.'

I fixed us both another large scotch. This, as best as I can recall it, is what he said:

4

'When we met before,' Marshall began, choosing his words carefully, 'I told you there were some people who were not too pleased about the things I knew.'

I acknowledged this.

'These people,' he went on, in the same deliberate tone, 'were not at all happy that they couldn't control this information in the way they wanted, but I assumed that if I took early retirement these people would leave me alone.'

'That was my understanding,' I said.

'Of course, I was not going to retire as such. I was, after all, only in my mid-forties, but I thought I could safely move to another part of the country, take up a new line of work, and put the past behind me.' He smiled at me with a certain shrewdness. 'Isn't that what we dream about all our lives? The idea that we can draw a line under our old selves and be born again.'

'The dream of leaving,' I murmured, the Pan Am ticket desk in my mind's eye.

'I think I can say that I made as good a shot at starting again as anyone I know.'

Something distracted him. He stood up and went across to the window, pulling the drapes closer together, a man wrapping himself tightly in privacy.

'My wife and I have always been fond of the West Country. She loves the works of Thomas Hardy and there is nothing we like better than to make up a picnic and visit Casterbridge or Egdon Heath.'

Marshall, I remembered, enjoyed speaking in this composed manner.

'I'm not a great reader myself, Seymour, but I respect

52

my wife's taste. To cut a long story short, we decided to move to Dorset. It's a small county. I believed I could find work in any one of a dozen towns and then commute. So we sold our house in the province, said goodbye to our friends and came to settle here on the mainland. People understood that we'd had enough of the Troubles. I am certain that no one suspected the real reason for the move.' He smiled inwardly. 'I know how to cover my tracks.'

I nodded, to encourage him, but did not interrupt.

'I began to apply for jobs. I wasn't fussy or greedy. I just wanted to be useful. Then I discovered, Seymour, that my former masters were watching me.'

'How was that?'

'Whenever I went for an interview I would give my old department as a reference. Three times I sailed through the final interview only to find my application mysteriously, sometimes abruptly, rejected.'

Marshall opened his briefcase. 'Here's a sample. A letter from a headmaster of a minor public school. I'd applied to be the bursar.' He put on a pair of heavy-rimmed glasses and began to read. ' "Dear Major Marshall, Thank you for coming to see us etc., etc. New paragraph. I regret to inform you that we have decided, after all, not to fill the post at this time. Yours sincerely, Eric Bagnall." ' He thrust the letter aside with exasperation. 'Yet the man had more or less promised me the job. I realised then that I had to play the game their way.'

'You always were a good games player,' I said.

'I rewrote my curriculum vitae, deleting my Army references, and applied for the post of administrator at a private sanatorium near the Dorset coast. They were impressed by my military record and I was taken on there and then, no questions asked.' He drained his glass. 'I thought my troubles were over.'

He accepted my offer of a refill. When we had met

53

before he was an angry man looking for support, now there was an air of resignation about him.

'Looking back, I feel bad about what happened next. Everything seemed rosy. I was happy in my work. My wife was settled in our new home. Friends came to visit. The fear had gone out of our lives. I was going to Rotary. Margaret had joined the Garden Club. We were becoming pillars of the community. Then I made a silly mistake.'

Marshall paused to consider his story. He became reflective. 'You've left your wife, Seymour. You know about marriage. I'm devoted to Margaret, of course, and we've been together for years. But you know how it is. Especially when you meet a pretty girl and you seem to click.'

He sighed. I waited patiently. I had not forgotten, from our earlier encounter, his compulsive need to inflict his sufferings on me.

'Kate was a nurse, from Scotland. She worked at a nearby clinic. The medical profession is amazingly sociable. Often, I'd find myself almost the only man among several attractive women. The others used to joke about it, and to begin with that's all it was, a joke. If there had not been so much laughter between us it might, even now, have remained a secret.'

I have to admit he had my attention.

'Kate and I got along like a house on fire. Something to do with clan feeling, I imagine. I felt sorry for her. She was unhappily married to a fellow called Roberts, a bookseller. I shouldn't speak ill of the dead, but he was a bastard. Everyone knew about his philandering. At first I was just trying to cheer her up. Then we discovered it was getting serious.'

'I know how it is.'

He looked at me gratefully. 'It was terrible. I loved Margaret and I thought I loved Kate. I did not know what to do. Of course, as soon as I started showing interest in his wife, Roberts came back into the picture with a vengeance.

There was never exactly a row or a scene, but a lot of tears and late nights.' He gave a little laugh of embarrassment. 'I'm basically just a funny old soldier, a novice in the affairs of the heart. I was out of my depth.'

I believed Marshall's confession of innocence. His actorish gallantry would be the mannerism of a man for whom flirtation was a defensive ploy, not a strategy for seduction.

'I decided I had to end it,' he went on. 'Frankly, not much had happened, just a couple of nights kissing and cuddling and some silly, romantic talk. The irony is that when the Roberts business happened our affair, such as it was, had virtually ceased.'

I handed him the bottle and he poured a generous measure into his glass.

'You must keep patience with me for a moment,' he continued, 'because the next part of the story will appear to be a digression. You will come to see that it proves the conspiracy against me.'

I was sceptical. I had heard him in this vein before. I knew his penchant for make-believe. But I did not betray my doubts and let him go on. Now he pulled an envelope out of his briefcase, holding it from me in a clumsy effort to arouse my curiosity.

'Shortly after we had moved to Dorset I had a telephone call from an advertising agency. Would I agree to model some military kit for a new defence magazine? I was surprised to be approached and said so. I was told I had been recommended by former colleagues. Names were mentioned. It seemed to be above-board, and I suppose I was flattered. A day's work. They could offer two hundred and fifty quid.' He frowned at the memory. 'I was hard up. That's a lot of money to me. So I agreed.'

I could not help myself. 'What happened?'

'It was weird, Seymour. I should have smelt a rat at once. I went to this address in Weymouth. The 3-D Photographic Agency. The studio was up a flight of stairs, a room overlooking the promenade. The photographer was this pot-bellied queen in leather trousers. He made me put on commando fatigues, smear my face with camouflage and pretend to fire various new weapons. All I can remember is this seaside pansy telling me: "You want to kill. Kill for the camera." '

He pulled a sheaf of prints out of the envelope. I found it hard not to smile at the absurd poses and mock fierceness.

'If things had not turned out so badly, I might have found it funny too. Who says the camera never lies?'

I apologised. I had forgotten how prickly he could be. I handed the pictures back. He stared at the images of himself as a killer. 'Once I'd had my cheque, I thought no more about it. Then, a few months later, I was driving along the promenade, on my way to meet Kate. I got a terrific shock. The 3–D Photographic Agency had disappeared. I had to stop and double-check, but it was as though it had never been.'

He pointed to the photographs. 'It wasn't until recently that I discovered the real significance of these pictures.' He slipped them back into the envelope. 'I was down in the dumps when we first met, Seymour, but this year has been the worst of my life.'

For a moment I thought he was going to break down, but he took a gulp of scotch and carried on.

'So my affair with Kate came to an end. It was a difficult decision, but the right one. I'm pleased to say that we managed to stay on good terms. I was even helping her investigate a divorce on the grounds of mental cruelty. Ironically, we were both getting used to being "just good friends" when we were thrown together again by that television show. You know, the Book Bash.'

I nodded unconvincingly.

At this point I should say that my neglect of Marshall's story was highly embarrassing to me. With Ruth, I had done my best to steer clear of the subject. I was only too acutely aware of what I had not done for Marshall, and

Ruth's potential reproach was more than I could stand.

'The show's become very popular,' said Marshall, noticing my ignorance. He explained that the Book Bash was a television programme which toured the country auctioning books and manuscripts on behalf of various worthy causes. Fashionable writers were invited to act as pundits, and the whole thing was sponsored by local businesses.

When the Book Bash came to the West Country, Marshall, the community honcho, became involved. 'My wife loves books – and so does Kate.' He paused. 'And Jeffrey Roberts was one of the main organisers, naturally.' I could see memories troubling him. 'In my naïve way, I thought that working together might help all of us.'

The telephone rang. I went into the kitchen. It was Ruth. 'Our mutual friend is here,' I said. 'Could we talk later?'

I came back into the living-room. Marshall was pacing in front of the electric fire. He looked at me. 'Do you think I would murder Kate's husband?'

I was taken aback. It was such a direct, almost intimate, question. 'No – no, of course not.' It was a glib response and I could see he was disappointed in me. 'Why should you? Your affair was over. It would make no sense, unless . . .'

He shook his head. 'I've already told you I love my wife.'

'And I believe you.'

He seemed relieved. 'Thank you.' He sat down, calmer again. 'Here's what happened. Judge for yourself. A few weeks ago, there was a farewell dinner organised by the Book Bash people. Margaret and I were invited of course, and so were Kate and Jeffrey. There was some question whether Roberts could make it, but finally the word came that he would be there. The restaurant was one of those country house affairs, with private suites as well as a public dining-room. I suppose there must have been twenty people

57

sitting round the table. You know how those television people like to eat. We had drinks and took our places. No sign of Roberts. Inevitably, there were a few raised eyebrows. I noticed that Kate was unhappy about her husband's absence and on the spur of the moment I volunteered to go and look for him. So I took the car, drove to their bungalow, and then to his shop. I could find no sign of him. I must have been away just over an hour. I'm afraid to say we all blamed Jeffrey's unreliability. Well, we finished the meal, and then Margaret and I went home. Kate had a lift from the producer. I thought no more about it until lunchtime the next day when Kate called me at the office in a terrible state. Some fishermen had pulled a body out of the sea that morning. The police had provisionally identified it as Roberts.' He paused. Marshall was never one to waste a good line. 'They were treating the case as murder.' He gave me that doomed-dog look again. 'And from the very beginning, I was their chief suspect.'

The phone rang again.

In some irritation, I hurried to answer it. 'Beaver here,' said a familiar voice.

5

This time I did not postpone the conversation. Whatever I might have felt about my father as a man, there are obligations to the dying. No one had any idea how long he would last. I had to assume he could go at any time, though in the end he proved as resilient as we might have expected.

The Beaver was never the kind to phone for a chat. His calls were brief and functional, conducted in the spirit of one used to giving orders. Tonight, his message was an invitation to spend Christmas Day with him. I said I was happy to accept, though I could not speak for Ruth. I would have to ask her and get back to him. I knew from his reaction that he disapproved of my acquiescence towards anything that smacked of feminism and women's lib. But I was also well aware that his curiosity about Ruth would overcome any lurking objections. He would be happy to await her reply. He had always been one for the ladies.

As we spoke, I could hear Marshall pacing about the front room. I wished I could talk more freely and at greater length. The major's visit had started so many hares in my mind. There were also questions I wanted to put to my father, but they would have to wait. As I put the phone down, my thoughts returned briefly to Ruth. We were supposed to be joyfully united at last, and yet, speaking objectively, my first action that evening had been to put her, metaphorically, on 'hold'.

When we were conducting our affair in secret, meeting in foreign places, surrendering to a two- or three-day fantasy, I had been strongly attracted to Ruth's elusiveness, her refusal to be pinned down, her mischievous love of escape. She offered the kind of challenge I did not have with Lizzie. Now that I had moved across the Atlantic, I wanted more commitment, and her refusal to compromise her freedom (what she called her 'space') was a source of growing inner disappointment. When I had said 'Could we talk later?' it was not merely because I was hooked by Marshall's story. I also wanted to say: I, too, must have my own space, thank you.

I was upset with her in another sense. Paradoxically, though I was becoming fascinated by his predicament, I resented Marshall's intrusion. Ruth had given him my address. She had, as it were, sent him to me. Why? To rub his misfortunes in my face? She could have told me herself. As I discovered later, she had most of the details at her journalistic fingertips.

This line of speculation reawoke other, darker thoughts. It was Ruth, of course, who had been responsible for bringing him into my life in the first place. What, exactly, was her relationship with him? What was her motive? Whose side was she on? Ruth is someone whose taste for mischief and adventure makes her dangerously unreliable. She will do things for the hell of it, to see what will happen next. A free spirit, if you like. Ordinary mortals tangle with such people at their peril.

In retrospect, if there was a moment when I began to realise that my hopes for our relationship were doomed it was during that evening with Marshall. Why do I say that so confidently? It is because the moment Marshall stepped into my living-room he was putting me inexorably into conflict with all that was closest to me at that time.

Worst of all, he put me in conflict with myself. I wanted to say: Go away. Leave me alone. But to do that would be to fail Ruth and to fail myself. In Ruth's eyes, Marshall was offering me the chance to win my spurs. It was an opportunity she constantly urged me to seize. She, after all, was the no-hostage-taking hard hitter who met all comers and won.

Those wide, bright eyes had pierced the toughest of defences. Yet, when I challenged her to take up Marshall's case herself her response was sheer Lady Macbeth. 'When you durst do it, then you were a man.'

She knew only too well that the promise I had made to Marshall was the ultimate challenge to myself. To let her step in and take over would be to surrender to her completely, to fail, and so to lose her. It would also involve losing control of a story about my father that, unconsciously, one way or another, I knew I had to tell.

I remember a conversation I had with my father in the days when as a teenager I used to visit him in the summer, an annual trip. I was full of adolescent rage, and about to take my mother's name as part of that defiance. At home, in eighth grade, I would boast about my father's secret life, invent James Bond exploits for him he never could have performed, and create an air of daredevil mystery. Here, at his table, surrounded by family heirlooms, watched by my ancestors, I would accuse him of making a living out of treachery. It was callow stuff and he was always surprisingly good-humoured about it, an elephant with a gnat. On this occasion I had said that his life was so full of betrayal, how could he bear to live with himself? He must, I said, in words that now seem prophetic, be eaten up inside.

'If only the world was, morally speaking, so simple, dear boy.' He loved to tease my American pomposity. 'Betray, of course, is an interesting word. It has two quite different meanings, offering two quite different interpretations. It can mean to uncover, but it can also imply concealment. And life is like that, full of double meanings. Nothing, I fear, is as simple as we would wish.'

61

6

Marshall was playing solitaire. He looked up from the cards as I came back, but said nothing. I apologised for the interruption, but did not explain it. I wanted to keep my father out of the equation for as long as possible.

'Patience.' He shuffled the pack together. 'Margaret taught me. I don't know what I would have done without her. She has stood by me through thick and thin. I had no right to that loyalty. I don't suppose you have any idea what kind of pressure I've been under.'

'I guess not.'

'Those tabloid journalists are jackals. Once they get hold of a story they chew it to the bone. Suddenly, the business with the photographs was explained. From nowhere it seemed, there were these pictures of me looking like a man who settled scores with violence.'

'Don't you have an alibi?'

'Not for an hour I don't. How long does it take to kill a man and dump his body in the sea?'

'No one saw you?'

'It was after dark. The house and the bookshop were deserted. I spoke to no one. I was in a hurry to get back to the dinner. During that hour, it seems, I could have been anywhere.'

I was curious. 'Are you frightened?'

It was a cruel question, but his response was surprisingly mild. 'You know, Seymour, I have been expecting this. I feel as though I have finally met my doom.' He looked at me strangely, and again there was that heaviness of speech. 'You know as well as I do that these people will not rest until I have been humiliated and destroyed.'

I have always been fascinated by the workings of fate and our attitude towards it. Marshall had the air of a man looking for punishment.

I attempted to rally his spirits. There was only an inquest, adjourned for technical reasons. There were no charges, and apparently no witnesses. If he was innocent, his attorney would prove his case.

He shook his head. 'I know I am done for,' he repeated, with that accusing note in his voice. 'Miscarriages of justice are a British trademark, especially when it comes to Ireland.'

'Don't you think you're in danger of getting things out of proportion?'

His anger was closer to the surface than I had ever seen before. 'If anything makes me get things out of proportion, Seymour, it's bloody Yanks who won't recognise their responsibilities.'

I've had this, on and off, over the years. It's something I've learned to live with. Of course, I'm on both sides of the fence, but Marshall always treated me as if I was Apple Pie and Old Glory all in one. I guess he wanted to differentiate me from the Beaver.

'The sins of the fathers . . .' I murmured, making a play for lightness.

'It's typical,' he said, almost to himself. Now he was speaking his mind. 'You come over here with smiles and dollars wanting to be our friends and then, as soon as the Old World starts to look a bit nasty, you're off, back to the other side of the pond, as you call it. And you just don't want to know. We could be on another planet. If that's moral responsibility, give me Perfidious Albion any day.'

He walked across to the window and stared out into the street. I knew he was annoyed with himself for his loss of control. He turned and began again in another mood.

'I realise, Seymour, that despite your background you cannot really understand my situation. When we met before

I painted a picture of bureaucratic infighting. I was trying to convince myself that it was only office politics. I was wrong. It is not a game, it's a war, and somewhere in the thick of the fighting is the tattered flag of class struggle.'

I have sometimes, to annoy my American friends, claimed that we, in the US, can exhibit class snobbery just like the Brits, though in a subtler way. I've had dinner tables resounding angrily with pat phrases about 'the society of opportunity' but now, listening to Marshall, I realised that such discussions were strictly for the debating chamber. What he was expressing was something I would never fully grasp.

'I was, and I still am, an outsider,' he was saying. 'I use odd words and have a funny accent. To English eyes, there is something slightly thuggish about the Scots. Perhaps that's why they often get us to do their dirty work. But when I started asking awkward questions about what I was being asked to do, then I was this tiresome Jock who had to be silenced.'

On the few occasions I had been with Marshall, I found that sooner or later his clannish nature would emerge. His resentment of the English, of whom my father was such a typical representative, was a splinter under his skin. I wondered why he had not retired to Scotland. The South seemed an odd (I think I said 'surprising') choice.

'I hoped I could forget myself by the sea.' Marshall was looking directly at me. 'Now I see that subconsciously I was saying to my enemies: I will live in your midst. I will not go away.'

There was something here I did not trust. 'Who exactly are your enemies now?' I could not prevent a note of sarcasm creeping into my question.

'Don't play games with me, Seymour. This has become a matter of life and death.'

I hesitated to reply. I wondered, if I stayed quiet, whether the Beaver's name would be mentioned. But Marshall could be stubborn too. Finally, I said: 'That was my father on the phone.'

'I'd figured as much.'

'I will probably spend Christmas with him,' I said. 'I expect your name will come up.'

He looked at me like a traveller searching for a flight that has already departed. 'Are you going to help?'

'I will talk to my father.' I stood up, to close the evening. 'So perhaps,' I went on, 'we should meet again in the New Year.' I opened the door and the cold air rushed in. 'Before the inquest.'

He seemed satisfied. His trip had not been wasted. We went through the ritual of exchanging phone numbers and addresses.

'Happy Christmas, Seymour.'

'Merry Christmas.' I did not feel happy or merry, and I could not bring myself to use his first name.

I watched him to the corner of the street, a lone, deliberate figure with a heavy back. Did a shadow move? I cannot say.

7

When I remember my father's house at Christmas that year I see ground-frost and winter sunshine. He and I are standing together on the terrace, looking down the estuary towards the English Channel. We do not speak, but we are close. Ruth is on the lawn in front of us, playing with the dog. Beyond the rhododendrons the tide is at the flood and a long finger of sea draws the eye towards the glittering horizon. I am conscious that I may not enjoy such a moment again.

The house was built by one of Nelson's admirals, returning from the Napoleonic Wars with a heap of prize money. My father always looked quite at home in a Regency setting and, although he never had much use for the formal rooms, the nautical associations of the place appealed to him. Before the final months of his illness, he would spend many happy hours pottering in the garden, or gossiping with the neighbours, and watching the ships in the harbour. My father was an essentially solitary man who liked to offer occasional, but splendid, hospitality.

Ruth, it turned out, was delighted to accept his invitation. Frankly, she was intrigued. She came back to London on Christmas Eve, bursting with news of her trip round Europe. Her life, I noted with envy, was in stark contrast to my own. She seemed to have an 'in' with so many people, diplomats, journalists and politicians. As an Australian, she was oblivious to those invisible national barriers that can inhibit Europeans. I suspect that they, in turn, found her a breath of fresh air, a sexy woman of verve and intelligence.

I have never wanted to undress a woman and make love to her the way I did with Ruth. Once or twice, during her frequent returns, I found myself wondering if this was solely my privilege. I was philosophical: so long as I didn't know, I believed I could accept that she might want to play away from time to time. She always came home to me. Besides, I might want my own freedom, sooner or later. I never anticipated, of course, the terms on which such a moment would finally materialise.

That Christmas Eve, she came breezing back into my life with a house-warming present from Paris, a model of the Eiffel Tower. 'A Gallic symbol for you,' she said, touching my trousers with a smile. I have it still. She also had a whole Camembert and a bottle of duty-free claret. We were in bed, enjoying the wine and cheese, when she said: 'So how was the major?'

'Paranoid.'

Ruth could never resist a gag. 'Just because he's paranoid, it doesn't mean they aren't out to get him.'

'He certainly seems to be in trouble.'

She became serious. 'If he hadn't lied to the police, things might be easier for him.'

'He lied to the police?'

'Didn't he tell you?'

I shook my head.

'He's ashamed, but he shouldn't be. He lied for love. To protect his wife. When they asked him about Kate, the dead man's wife, he denied they had ever had an affair.'

I looked at her in amazement. 'They could go to town with evidence like that.'

'He says he panicked.'

'I'd say he was too accident-prone for his own good.'

I was affronted that Marshall should have decided to keep this detail from me, and fell silent. I had been hoping we might have a lazy, carefree holiday, but he was intruding again like the Ghost of Christmas Past.

Ruth knew what I was thinking. 'Why can't you admit that Marshall is part of our lives, whether you like it or not?'

'Miss Moral High Ground rides again.'

She jumped out of bed and went angrily to the bathroom. Although we both left the subject of Marshall severely alone for the rest of the evening, there was still a tension in the air when we set off on Christmas morning to drive to my father's.

Ruth knew the printed facts about the Beaver and I had spoken about him from time to time, but today she was in a quizzing mood. I was quite willing to talk about my father if it kept the atmosphere between us even-tempered, though there would always be some areas I preferred to keep to myself.

I forget, until I start to go over his career, how long ago he left the Royal Navy. He used to style himself Admiral when it pleased him, but he exchanged his uniform for a suit more than ten years back. I was in the middle of my disastrous year at Oxford, a botched attempt at an English education from which I fled after three terms, when he became an unconventional member of a surprisingly unconventional English club, the Civil Service.

Civil servants are often described as 'faceless', but this is a newspaper term, an adjective I might have used in a speech to stir the voters' fears of the things that go on behind closed doors in the corridors of power. The government officials I met with my father were amongst the most eccentric individuals I have ever encountered. It was as though the anonymity of their profession gave them the freedom to let their true natures flourish unhindered. They pursued odd hobbies, belonged to odd societies and, in several cases, conducted surprisingly odd private lives. Americans who came across these people simply could not believe they were, so to speak, in charge of anything.

My father fitted into this world perfectly. He celebrated eccentricity. He liked the idea of things being not what they seemed. I was, I fear, something of a disappointment to him, a squeaky-clean, dime-a-dozen American kid stuffed with conventional opinions, as alien as a green-skinned visitor from outer space. If I had turned round and told him I was supporting the Vietnam War, let the Pentagon bomb the hell out of Hanoi and eliminate Ho Chi Minh, then perhaps I might have attracted his attention.

I've mentioned that people were inclined to put him in the wrong pigeonhole, but the mistake was hardly surprising. The Beaver seemed to be part of that running conversation the British establishment has with itself. He seemed to know everyone, and be everywhere. He was, and loved to be, a fixer, a troubleshooter. From time to time, they would send him to some farflung hotspot, to write a confidential report or conduct a secret meeting with a guerrilla commander. He would play the game called Imperialism once again. I'm told he did it brilliantly. He would still receive Christmas cards from people he bumped into years ago, people from all over the world who couldn't forget him and wanted to keep in touch.

Even then, he was a lone wolf. He was on nobody's team, though he could give a good impression of being a team player. Politically, he defied classification. I am sure his colleagues thought he was conservative, but did not know he supported nuclear disarmament. Others may have imagined him a liberal democrat but overlooked the fact that he believed in a strong central government. He was the kind of person, if I may put it in American terms, who would have signed the Declaration of Independence but defended slavery.

My mother came from a Southern family for whom such contradictions were meat and drink. She was born into a society that was still reminiscent of *Gone With the Wind*. I believe my father swept her off her feet. She was, unconsciously no doubt, looking for such a man. She was this adventure-seeking American girl of twenty-three who had virtually run away from home to go with the troops to Europe. Her parents were anxious but secretly pleased. They were that sort of family, rebels with a taste for the unusual.

My grandfather, a member of the Committee for National Morale, was delighted to hear that his daughter had, as he put it, 'bagged a Brit'.

The 'Brit' in question was not yet thirty, but the fortunes of war would soon give him the command of a destroyer. He was good-looking in an unshaven, slightly haggard way, and as a youthful seadog with experience of battle the object of much female attention on shore. He was already 'the Beaver'.

They fell for each other at first sight. Even by the standards of wartime theirs was a whirlwind romance. I was conceived before they were married. Miss Betty Gilchrist became Mrs Ronald Lefevre in a chilly parish church a few months before VE Day. The honeymoon was a long weekend in the Lake District. They had known each other for a matter of weeks.

I was nine when the whirlwind finally blew itself out. My mother and I came back to the United States and I began to turn into a sort of American. That was when I decided to become a Gilchrist, a filial protest in which Mother cheerfully acquiesced.

In the beginning, after the separation, a pretence was made at a transatlantic relationship and I was encouraged to observe neutrality. But, living with my mother, a strong-willed, articulate woman, I soon found I was having to take sides, if only to offer moral support. Besides, it was hard to excuse my father's behaviour. During my teenage years, he became a stranger, or worse, an acquaintance. I hardly knew him, and what I knew I despised.

I cannot think of those times without feeling again the hot plastic seats of the school bus on the back of my bare legs or seeing again my mother buying ice-cream and hamburgers at the local gas station. I was proud to be a young American, proud to repeat the Pledge of Allegiance every morning, and proud to say or do anything that set me apart from my father and his world.

That, I suppose, was why I flunked Oxford. I had no sympathy for the place or its requirements and traditions.

The students seemed stuck-up and childish, openly contemptuous of outsiders and emotionally backward, tight-assed as only the English can be. I couldn't wait to get out, and it gave me extra satisfaction to give two fingers to my father's alma mater and quit.

At first, I was happy to go over this ground, but the deeper Ruth pressed into my family history, the more reluctant I became. There were things here I did not wish to speak about, at least not yet, and certainly not then. I had conflicting obligations.

Secretly, I half wanted the car to break down on the freeway, but that pretext was denied. It was midday when we turned up the steep, wooded drive.

The Beaver was waiting for us. He had lost weight, as he had warned me, and walked with a stick, but there was still life in his stride as he came to greet us.

' "My name is Ozymandias, king of kings, look on my works, ye Mighty, and despair . . ." Sam Gilchrist!' He embraced me and turned to Ruth. 'Miss Ritchie!' He made a kind of theatrical bow. ' "Round the decay of this colossal wreck, boundless and bare, the lone and level sands stretch far away." A pleasure to meet you.'

Ruth was laughing as they shook hands, and I knew at a glance that, whatever reservations she might have harboured in advance, she was, temporarily at least, enchanted.

My father stood in front of us, presenting arms with his stick. He is tall and sun-tanned. He has the face of a man who has spent many long watches scanning the horizon for enemy ships. 'Well then, Gilchrist, how do I look?'

How could I forget the swank and swagger of the man! It was typical of him to upstage his guests. 'You're looking pretty good,' I said, and I meant it. 'Are you still having the treatment?'

'No escaping it, dear boy. My quack's gone skiing for Christmas, but he wants to see me in the New Year. With any luck I'll be dead by then.'

He was clowning, of course. There never was a man who celebrated his hold on life as tenaciously as my father. Now he was showing off his house to Ruth and she was making enthusiastic noises. The dog appeared and Ruth, who loves animals, ran playfully onto the lawn with it.

I looked at my father, encouraged by the general air of good humour. 'Well, what do you think?'

'I don't trust first impressions. I'll tell you after lunch. Nice figure.' He pointed with his stick. 'D'you see? We have *Ark Royal* with us for the New Year.'

I shaded my eyes against the sun and the water and thought: Will this be the last time?

Ruth came up, with the dog bouncing round her. She was slightly breathless. She kissed me in that artless, affectionate way she had. 'It's wonderful, darling.' Her voice was full of reconciliation. 'Why didn't you tell me?'

I was about to answer when the french windows behind us opened with a squeak and a small, tired-looking woman in beige came out to join us.

My father turned, strangely gallant and remote. 'Jane, my dear. They've arrived.' He winked at Ruth. 'This is Jane,' he said. 'She looks after me and answers to my every whim, don't you, dear?'

Jane's smiling face was round and smooth and gave nothing away. 'Whatever you say, Admiral,' she said. 'Lunch is ready whenever you are.'

Ruth flashed me a look of curiosity and surprise, and I realised then that I had neglected to explain the intricacies of my father's domestic set-up.

8

Once my father was seated at the head of the table, it was as though nothing had changed. Behind him, great-grandfather Lefevre cast an imperious eye over the occasion from his favourite steed, as he had so often in the past. Each place was decorated with that quintessential British party favour, the Christmas cracker. Two ruby decanters and the fruit bowl were loaded ready for action on the sideboard. Outside, the winter air was still.

We pulled the crackers, put on the paper hats, and Jane served, as she always did, while my father provided the conversational hors d'oeuvres, as he always did. I might have been sixteen or seventeen. Today, delighted to have a new audience, he was addressing himself to Ruth. It was, perhaps, the mark of his illness that he did not flirt with her as outrageously as he might have done in the past.

'The posh term for my condition is carcinoma of the prostate.'

I exchanged a look with Jane. Only my father could boast about his failing prostate gland.

'My doctors say they have it under control, but that means they have me under control as well.' He lifted the wine out of the basket in front of him. 'The vino, in your honour, my dear, is a Coonawarra Cabernet Sauvignon.' He studied the label with approval, a scholar with a rare text. 'Lake's Folly, nineteen seventy-three. An interesting year.' There was a satisfying glug-gulp as he tipped the bottle. 'The truth is my balls are shrinking and there's absolutely nothing I can do about it.' He raised his glass to savour the first taste. 'Another thing about this infernal disease is that you start to lose your marbles, or at least you think you do.'

'If you don't mind my saying so, Admiral, you seem pretty much all there.' Ruth was good at the direct, sympathetic line. 'Isn't there some alternative treatment?'

'What? In America or something? The short answer is No. I suppose I should be thankful for small mercies, in the old days they used to cut your balls off. Now I have to have these monthly injections. Hormone treatment, God help us.'

Jane, who had presumably heard all this a dozen times, went into the kitchen. My father lowered his voice. 'My advice to you two is have all the sex you can while you can get it.' I sensed he was getting into his stride. He leant towards Ruth. 'I tried to take a woman to bed the other day. Jane was away, visiting her daughter. I had the place to myself. You know me, Sam, improve the shining hour and whatnot.' His voice dropped to a stage whisper. 'I rang up an old flame. She comes over, hot to trot. What a fiasco! Nothing doing!'

I saw the dangerous light of candour in Ruth's eyes. 'Were you embarrassed?' she asked.

'Embarrassed! I was depressed. Imagine.'

'Perhaps it was your old flame who was not quite up to the knocker in the bedroom department,' said Ruth.

My father looked at her with surprise and was about to reply when Jane returned from the kitchen with the sauce-boat and took her place across the table.

There was an awkward pause and then we began to eat. Ruth, sensing my father's egotism, launched into another fascinated question about his treatment. I turned to Jane and asked about Susan.

'She is not well at the moment,' she murmured.

'I'm sorry.' I did not know what else to add. I felt stiff and uneasy. I was anxious that our conversation should remain discreet.

My father, at the other end, had been giving Ruth a detailed run-down of his symptoms. She said something and he laughed. 'Excellent joke, my dear. D'you hear that, Gilchrist? "Prostate, c'est moi." I like a witty woman.'

Ruth flashed her conquering smile down the table. Jane and I did our best to share the merriment.

My father put his knife and fork down to survey the festive board. 'A superlative bird,' he announced, raising his glass for a toast.

'Happy hols,' said Ruth, belligerently secular.

'Happy Christmas to you both,' I said, with a smile in Jane's direction.

'Here's to absent friends,' said my father, looking squarely at me.

I was afraid he might mention Lizzie and the kids and even Mother by name, but I think there was something about Ruth's presence that inhibited him.

I kept my defences ready, nonetheless. I had names of my own with which I could retaliate, the names I remembered from my teenage years, Emma Carteret, Judy Woodhead, and Camilla Wilson-Booth, to mention three of the most notable.

When I was eleven or twelve, the women in my father's life were known as Aunty this or that, but as soon as I was a teenager all such pretence was abandoned. I saw these women with my inner eye, laughing, flirtatious, indulgent, gorgeous women in clouds of perfume, women who petted me, gave me presents, confided to me, women who shimmered through a summer dusk of memory in whispering silks.

Jane, fast-forwarding the conversation with her usual tact, asked me what I would be doing in London. I began to explain my plans for the agency.

'Public relations,' interrupted my father, in a withering summing-up. 'That's all people think about these days, the triumph of image over reality.'

'Give me image any day,' said Ruth. 'Look at you, Admiral. The picture of health.' She gave one of her saloon-bar laughs. 'I don't want to know that you can't get it up any more.'

My father looked at Jane, a naughty schoolboy watching matron's eye, but she seemed not to care. It was not as though she had not heard this sort of thing here before.

'Thank you, my dear, for those kind words of sympathy.' I looked at my plate. My father's libido was now a shadow of its former self, but it was not entirely extinguished.

There was a momentary lull and then I heard myself addressed in the mildest of conversational gambits. 'One person who could do with some public relations is that President of yours, Sam. What's going to happen to him? He seems to have made a fairly good hash of things.'

I replied that the polls showed people rallying to him over the hostage crisis. 'He's not done such a bad job.'

'I've spoken to people in Europe and Washington who say he'll get a second term,' added Ruth.

'I wouldn't bet on it,' he replied.

'I would,' she said, putting out her right hand. 'Ten bucks.'

She was flirting with him, and he was loving it. 'Shake,' he said. 'I like a gambling girl.'

'You're our witness, Sam,' said Ruth.

'Sure,' I replied, wondering exactly what I was witnessing.

'Well,' said my father cheerfully, 'I hope I'll be around to see this famous second term.'

'We'll keep you going, Admiral,' said Ruth, 'one way or another.'

Jane was not enjoying this, either. She got up to clear the plates, and I helped her gladly. In the kitchen she said: 'Ruth seems very lively.'

We smiled at each other. I did not want to talk about Ruth.

I resented the fact that my father was responding to her sex-appeal, to her calculated outrageousness. It had always been my secret fear that he was the more desirable. Is it inevitable that fathers and sons shall always see each other as rivals?

I said: 'Where is Susan today?'

'She's back in care, I'm afraid. They have to keep her under observation while they adjust the medication.' Jane nodded towards the door. 'Does she – ?'

'She doesn't,' I said. 'I thought . . .'

We were great ones for the unfinished sentence, Jane and I.

'Thank you,' she said, and she took my hand. Her fingers were ruddy with cleaning and dish washing. 'There's time enough, no doubt.'

My father's nautical tones boomed indistinctly in the background.

'How is he, really?'

'He's not been too good. He's putting on a show today, as you'd expect, but he'll pay for it tomorrow. He gets easily tired.'

Through the open door I could hear Ruth laughing, and I knew instinctively that my father was telling risqué stories. Apart from chasing women, he was at his happiest when he was back in the wardroom with his men, and Ruth was always glad to be one of the boys.

I raised the Christmas pudding, haloed in blue flame, and carried it before me, making a mock fanfare as I came into the dining-room. This was the Lefevre family ritual.

The Beaver applauded and began to sing in a quavering tenor: 'Queen Victoria, Queen Victoria, Queen of England, Empress of India . . .'

He caught sight of Ruth's expression and stopped. 'An old naval song,' he explained. 'We used to sing it marching up and down the wardroom in dinner jackets.' He smiled. 'I suppose it must seem rather silly to you.'

'Take a careful squiz,' she said, wryly, 'and you'll see the chains round my ankles.'

'One of my best friends was an Australian,' said my father. 'He copped it in Korea.' He raised his glass. 'To the immortal memory of Peter –' He stopped. 'But I am forgetting myself again. Sam, dear boy, I have a rather special port – you will take a glass of port? – on the sideboard there, if you would care to do the honours. While for those who prefer something lighter there is some very agreeable Madeira.'

I placed both the decanters in front of him.

'Taylor Fifty-five,' he said, greeting an old friend with an anticipatory sniff.

It was as the port and Madeira were circulating that Ruth struck, as I had feared she would.

'If you'll excuse my directness, Admiral –'

'I rather like your directness, my dear.'

'It's not often I get the chance to check a story at source.'

My father was impatient with niceties. He waved her preamble aside. 'What do you want to know?'

'I want to know about Craig Marshall,' she said.

I have to hand it to the old boy. He didn't bat an eyelid. 'You mean the Book Bash murder chap?'

She nodded.

'An amazing story. I've been following it in the papers.'

'But you wouldn't have to follow it in the papers, surely? I mean, you do know Major Marshall?'

He gave her his best Ozymandias look. I've seen it a hundred times. It turns most people to stone. 'I knew him once, rather briefly.' He turned his stare coldly in my direction. 'As Sam has doubtless told you.'

It was typical that he should blame me. I wanted to deny the charge. I wanted to say that her information had come from Marshall. But I said nothing and Ruth, who was never lightly deterred, pressed on with her questions.

'You met Marshall in Northern Ireland, I believe?'

He became thoughtful. 'Let me see. It must have been seventy-two or seventy-three. Things were getting rough. I was sent over there to do a confidential report. Marshall was my minder. A bit army-barmy, as they say, but a nice enough chap.'

Ruth has no respect for, or perhaps even knowledge of, any tradition of reticence. She battled forward regardless. 'If you don't mind my asking, what exactly were you doing there?'

My father did not bluster, as he might have done in the past. He treated her question with seriousness. 'This is off the record, now. There were two departments. The usual thing. Left hand, right hand. I had to bang heads together and write a report. All very hush-hush. On the one hand this, on the other hand that. Marshall knew the ropes. He took me round.' He brightened. 'We played squash, I remember.'

'Is that all?'

'As far as I can recall.' He looked at me again. I think he was wondering if I would let him skate over this thin ice without comment. 'You meet an awful lot of people in my line of business. I couldn't be entirely certain.'

Ruth nodded, waiting for more.

'I don't know how he got mixed up in the Book Bash nonsense,' my father went on. 'Of course, nothing has been proved yet, but the press have certainly had a field-day. There's some story about an affair with the dead man's wife.' He smiled. 'As young Sam has finally discovered, people will do anything for love.'

Ruth was not disarmed by the smile. She was polite, but firm. 'I don't think you're telling us the full story, Admiral,' she said.

My father looked wounded for the first time, a stag at bay. I realised then how much weaker he had become.

I said: 'Let's change the subject.'

Ruth rounded on me. 'I don't see why. He agreed to discuss Marshall in the first place.'

Then we had an argument, the two of us, the argument we should have had the night before, right there at the table.

My father began to sing: 'Queen Victoria, Queen Victoria . . .'

Jane said: 'Ruth, dear, why don't you and I go and make

the coffee.' She was quite firm herself, when she needed to be, and Ruth did not argue.

I was alone with my old man at last.

9

I did not have to apologise for Ruth. My father was always indulgent towards representatives of the opposite sex who flirted as gamely as she had done. Anyway, his gratitude for my unexpected support at a difficult moment put me in automatic credit.

'She reminds me of your mother,' he said, as the door closed. 'Headstrong.' He tilted the decanter. 'Women,' he said, an experienced judge pronouncing one of his regular verdicts.

I felt as close to him then as I ever had. 'I wish,' I said, 'I wasn't so much in love.'

'If I was you, I'd enjoy it,' he replied, 'while it lasts.' He looked me in the eye. 'You won't keep her for long.'

'Thanks.' I was hurt, but I must have known that he was right because I did not argue with him.

'Whatever you do, don't marry her. The sexy ones never last, in my experience.'

I smiled. 'You've got sex on the brain.'

'The only place for it, the way I am now, God help me.'

He looked sad, a dog without a bone, and I felt sorry for him. My father always found the company of women more satisfying than men. After his marriage was over, he was lucky in his affairs. His mistresses were generally women who loved him and looked after him. Most of them treated me, when I was with him, as a son or a nephew or even, if I was lucky, as a younger brother.

No one, I believe, ever quite replaced my mother in his eyes. They still loved each other, though they were happier apart. He kept her picture, the wartime bride with the startled look of the young and newly married, by his bedside long after the other women had departed from sight and mind.

At home in Virginia she, too, has his picture, a young man in naval uniform, in a silver frame on her dressing-table. They did not see each other in twenty years, but they exchanged letters at Christmas and birthdays. He broke her heart when he left, but he was breaking it while he stayed. I sometimes wished they didn't have me to remind them of their moment of passion.

My mother nearly got remarried to one of our legislators, a boisterous power-broker from Atlanta. He looked good on paper, widowed with four children. After Watergate, he looked less good. Fortunately, she drew back at the last minute. I'm glad she kept her nerve.

Officially, my parents were divorced, but nothing, I believe, could have changed the way they felt about each other.

He guessed what I was thinking. 'Your mother says I should have a holiday in Bangkok and get laid pro-fessionally.'

I was not surprised. My mother was, like her husband, a very practical person, especially about sex. I asked him how much he had told her about his illness.

'Everything.' He pierced me with a look of painful can-dour. 'Why not? There's no percentage in hiding it from her, or from myself. I'm not asking for sympathy. I've had a good run. I'll be dead in three years, maybe less.'

'Is that what they say?'

'It's what I asked them to tell me.'

How typical, I thought, that he should be so matter-of-fact. He might have been discussing a colleague's life, not his own. I found myself feeling sorry for Jane.

'Are you afraid?'

He considered this. 'I'm afraid of the unknown, but also eager for it in a funny way. And I'm afraid of the pain, naturally.'

A companionable silence came between us, a silence in which my father offered me a Monte Cristo, which I refused. The obligations of hospitality satisfied, he lit one for himself with evident relish. The smoke billowed in front of him and I imagined him in the fog of battle on the deck of a seventy-four.

I could hear Ruth and Jane murmuring over the dishes in the kitchen and wondered, panicking slightly, what on earth they could be talking about. I hoped Ruth was respecting the delicacy of Jane's situation. Ruth did not like to be denied a clear picture. Here, where so much was unspoken, I feared she might be again provoked into further interrogation.

'Still happy to be my executor?'

My father's voice brought me back to the present moment. The light was going. We were sitting in twilight. The glowing stub of his cigar nodded in the shadow.

'Is your lawyer getting cold feet?'

'O'Reilly?' He gave a self-deprecating laugh. 'The first time I put the full tangle of my life before him I thought he was going to have a seizure.' He blew a confident puff of smoke in my direction. 'I'm glad to say he rallied well. The will reflects, I believe, the sensible, even witty, resolution of a complex situation. I am not, as I told you before, a rich man, but there's enough to go round. There'll inevitably be disappointment in some quarters, but *tant pis*.'

It was typical that my father should turn the writing of his will into something of an entertainment. 'Well, I need a bit of an incentive to make the new business pay,' I said, entering into the spirit of the conversation.

'I have been as generous as I can to your mother,' he went on, more thoughtfully, releasing another puff. 'If only . . .'

It was then that I wished I wasn't there to remind him of the past. 'You always taught me to have no regrets,' I said.

For a moment, he didn't reply, and I wondered if he had heard me.

'The worst of dying is what it does to your head,' he remarked finally. 'You're right to remind me. No regrets. That is my credo. I have tried to live my life to the full. I've taken every chance. I've slept with as many women as would let me. I've put my life in danger for my country and also just for the hell of it. What more could I have done?'

I sensed he wanted me to ask him about the past, but I could not bring myself to raise the subject. 'You couldn't,' I said.

'And now,' he went on, warming to his theme, 'here I am watching my life run out like sand in an hourglass. What's more, I feel so bloody helpless. I don't know exactly why, but I'm getting these absurd moments of guilt.'

There it was again, the invitation to press a question. 'What kind of guilt?'

'Anything and everything. Your mother, dear Jane, even you . . .'

He was soliciting my curiosity. Perhaps, after his exchange with Ruth, he felt slightly reckless.

The British ruling class survives on hypocrisy and self-confidence. In my experience, it is rare to find its representatives in such an open and expansive mood. I had to risk a rebuff. 'Do you think you could feel guilty about Craig Marshall?'

He frowned, but did not retaliate. 'Yes, I could feel guilty about Craig Marshall.'

'Is that so irrational?'

'For someone who fixed his new job it is.' He chucked his cigar into the fire. 'Marshall doesn't know that, of course. I'm speaking in confidence, Sam.'

My father loved to pull strings behind the scenes, just as, on his sickbed, he was pleased to be the star of the show.

I concealed my surprise, naturally. Very matter-of-fact I said: 'I feel I should do something like that, something useful to him.'

84

'Don't,' he said. 'These are dangerous waters.' He reached down for his stick. 'It isn't a good idea.' We had gone far enough down this road together and now he was warning me off.

'Why not?'

'It won't do you any good, old boy.' He put out his hand, and I helped him to his feet. 'Time to rejoin the ladies,' he said.

10

On New Year's Day I woke in Ruth's bed, so I suppose you can say we made up. I think my father, a veteran of the war between the sexes, had been amused to see his son taking some flak for a change.

Now the sun was up, subdued and pale, like a reveller with a hangover. I lay there, with the riot of Ruth's things around me, listening to Strauss waltzes, a live broadcast from Vienna. Ruth was mixing a champagne cocktail on the ironing board by the window. She was naked. We had just made love.

I looked at my watch. It was almost noon. The first day of the new decade. At home, it would be the year in which the President, my President, was swept from power by the angry forces of flag-waving Republicanism. He had injured the pride of our people and they were going to run him out of town. The high-rollers turned their backs on church-going, reverted to playing poker and put a movie star in charge of the casino.

Here, the Brits had exchanged the nanny state for Big Nanny herself, the Iron Lady. The first time I met Marshall he had talked about 'the rise of the Right' and I had assumed this was gossip from the officers' mess. Now I would have to admit, if the subject came up when we met again that afternoon, that I had been wrong, self-confidently wrong, as only the political analyst can be. The counter-revolution had begun. Victorian values were back in fashion. Hair was being worn short-back-and-sides. Somehow, it was appropriate that the BBC should be playing 'The Blue Danube', theme music for a new regime.

Ruth had planned the meeting with Marshall herself.

We were to go to Hampstead Heath and rendezvous by Jack Straw's Castle, like characters in a film. I remember getting there early and sitting in the car with yesterday's newspapers. The Soviets were consolidating their grip on Kabul. Another headache for the Old Man. What's that line? 'When sorrows come, they come not single spies, but in battalions.' In New York, the atmosphere of crisis had sparked off a scramble for gold. The price had soared to nearly six hundred dollars an ounce, and in Manhattan widows and wise guys were standing in line to cash in quick.

Marshall came up to the Volkswagen, as arranged. He glanced at the headlines. 'In time of trouble,' he said, with that Scottish pitch, 'we return to the essentials.' As I got out to shake his hand, he added: 'Man is still such a primitive animal.' He was dressed for the walk like an Edwardian mountaineer, and his skin was iron-grey in the cold. There was a shaving cut on his chin, a hint of vulnerability in a face that otherwise gave little away.

We set off, across the road and down the hill. There was frost on the grass and our breath was foggy. We passed couples walking their dogs and children playing among the bushes with toy guns. For a while we hardly spoke. I was glad to let the rhythm of our feet stimulate our thoughts collectively and bring us into a kind of harmony.

Ruth looked stunningly sexy that day, at least to me. She was wearing an explorer's anorak with a fur-trimmed hood, and rainbow coloured leggings. Next to Marshall, she moved with a dancer's step. She had slipped her arm into his, for friendship, and perhaps to put him at ease. On this occasion I did not worry, as I had worried before, about the nature of their relationship.

We had been walking for some minutes when finally I said: 'I did speak to my father at Christmas.'

Ruth let out a yell of delight. 'You should have seen them in action, Craig. The charge of the silver spoon brigade.'

I hated her assumption that I was my father's son, but I kept my peace and smiled non-committally.

Ruth holds the view (I call it a conspiracy theory) that all the people who matter in England went to the same school. In her demonology, the life experience of the English élite is a kind of prolonged adolescence in which, psychologically speaking, they remain in some kind of mental and emotional dorm. I like to believe that when I became a Gilchrist I said goodbye to all that, but Ruth disagrees.

Marshall was diplomatic. 'How was your father?'

'He remembers you well,' I said.

'We played squash,' Marshall replied, his interest pricked. 'He almost beat me.'

I smiled. 'He was interested to hear that you and I had met up.'

'I'm sure it came as no surprise.'

'No, I don't suppose it did.'

I went back over some of the details of the visit in my mind, details I had not mentioned to Ruth. I had been asked to supply the registration number of my car, and my passenger's name and address, twenty-four hours in advance. The two men in green parkas we had met as we came up the drive were not, as I had claimed, local farmers, but part of the permanent watch on the house mounted by the Special Branch. My father was retired, but he was still a terrorist target. I had to acknowledge there would always be more to his life than he was prepared to let on, especially to his own flesh and blood.

Marshall quickened his step. We were climbing a slope towards a clump of trees. At the top, he rested and looked about. He was still remarkably fit. He was, I noticed, hardly out of breath. Through the pale blue frosty light, we had a panoramic view of London, from the docklands to the Post Office Tower.

'A great city is so vulnerable,' said Marshall reflectively.

'A few bombs, or even bomb scares, and it becomes a ghost town. Were you here in seventy-four?'

'Briefly.'

'The powers that be almost lost control of the situation.'

'I remember.' I had visited my father with my young family that year. Alice was two, Charlie four. Even the irrepressible Beaver was concerned. 'Hunting terrorists on the mainland,' he announced, 'is like looking for gnat-shit in a pepperpot.'

'That was when we began to go off the rails,' said Marshall, turning away from the view. 'I've never put my finger on it, but that was when something went wrong, seriously wrong.'

'What kind of something?'

'A loss of nerve, perhaps.' The Highland accent gave his words an extra spin. 'When we first met,' he said, 'I think I told you that Northern Ireland had become an adventure playground for men who had never grown up, men who could not stop themselves looking for a thrill or two.'

I nodded. I remembered him saying something of this sort.

'You,' he went on, 'you're a sensible person. You and all the other sensible people want to see the problem settled, sensibly. The types I'm talking about actually welcomed the conflict. It gave them a chance to play truant from ordinary life.' He touched my arm to emphasise his point. 'I know what I'm talking about. I had this experience myself. Everyone goes a little bit crazy over there.'

Two men in lumpy anoraks walked past, apparently in conversation. Marshall paused to watch them go by, but made no comment.

'A weird kind of escapism,' I said.

'Weird and dangerous,' he replied. 'It gives you ideas. It gives you a taste for the unacceptable.'

'My father would have appreciated that,' I said, smiling inwardly at the idea.

He ignored this, rather too deliberately I thought. 'Then

all at once you find the games you enjoyed in the adventure playground are being played rather closer to home and you start to panic.'

'And did they?'

'Look at me.' Marshall put his hand on his heart, a gesture of melodrama I have come to associate with him. 'I am the evidence of their panic. They would never have done what they've done to me now if I wasn't an embarrassing reminder of things they wished they could deny.'

'You're very sure about this.'

'I have every right to be, for Christ's sake.'

He hated his story to be doubted, and I apologised.

He looked at me. 'Imagine a man with a malignant tumour. If he doesn't cut it out, who knows where it will spread next?'

I was never sure how much Marshall intended, but I was always impressed by the skill with which he managed to get under my skin. 'Perhaps it will go to his brain and drive him mad,' I said, and I saw my father lying in the coma of imminent death.

'Exactly,' he replied with satisfaction. 'I am the evidence of that madness.'

When Marshall resorted to utterances such as these I remembered why I distrusted his claims. I said: 'My father says you were a good soldier.'

I could see he was intrigued by my conversation with the Beaver.

'What else did he say about me?'

Ruth jumped in. 'It was what he didn't say that was most revealing.'

I had to control myself here. If I wasn't careful, she and I would have another argument, a repeat performance.

'He wanted to know when the inquest was to be, and what the issues were,' I said.

'He would know those well enough, but I suppose he was just checking how much I'd told you,' he replied.

90

I always sensed, with Marshall, that he had to control the terms of every exchange. If information was his currency, he was in his own way a miser.

I found myself wanting to discompose him. 'Why didn't you tell me you lied to the police?'

'I felt foolish,' he replied. 'I still do. Foolish and ashamed.' He turned towards Ruth. Now he was vulnerable, an actor without a script. 'Whatever the future holds, they will have broken me.'

Ruth put her arm round him. 'Come on, Craig.'

'No, I can admit it. I fought them and they won. The minute I made that lie I knew I had lost.' He looked at me coldly. 'Your father knows all this.'

'That's your assumption,' I said.

'Come on, Sam darling, of course he knows.' Ruth was on Marshall's side and I was watching my temper again.

'Think about it, Seymour.' Marshall was challenging me once more. 'Don't tell me he didn't warn you to stay out of this.'

I could hardly deny it. I heard my father's voice: 'It won't do you any good, old boy.'

Marshall was getting even. 'The trouble is, Seymour, that for better or worse, you have a conscience. It was this conscience of yours that stopped you pushing the case against your old man. And it was this conscience of yours, plus a little nagging from this young lady, that encouraged you to get in touch with me. Now you're back in the frame.' His smile was punitive. 'Sorry about that, Seymour.'

I knew this as well as anyone. Whatever skills I have in the world of affairs, in this particular narrative I am essentially a coward. There is nothing the coward fears like uncertainty. I found myself wondering what protection my relationship with my father afforded me. For a moment I was sorry I wasn't still in America.

Ruth echoed my thoughts. In retrospect, her words may

have expressed an unconscious wish. 'I told you it was a risk to come here.'

'If I wasn't here, I wouldn't be with you, darling,' I said, putting my arm around her.

'That may be my bad luck,' said Marshall, and the twist of his laughter turned inside me like a knife.

'Whatever happens,' said Ruth, staring at me hard and provocatively, 'we'll stand by you.'

'Will I see you at the inquest?'

'Of course,' she said.

I was silent. Marshall looked at me, still challenging. 'And you, Seymour?'

'My father has cancer,' I said. 'He could die soon.'

Marshall turned away without a word, striding down the hill. Ruth and I followed, at a distance.

We did not speak.

11

I think I gave the new business my best shot. I spent real money to make the front office reassuring to potential clients. Ah, the balm of the rubber plant and the hunting print! I hired a secretary, Rosemary, fresh out of typing school, living-at-home-with-Mummy-and-Daddy, and only too eager to please. I also prepared a promotional brochure featuring my work for the President of the United States. I cannot read this now without embarrassment.

In retrospect, my American connections were my undoing. The more I rang my contacts, touting for work, the more I became in demand as 'a source' on the disintegrating White House. A few people wanted my business, but the vast majority would call me for a quote from 'a former White House aide'. I thought that getting my name in the paper would establish my credentials and help pay the rent. I could not have been more mistaken.

Apart from the continuing saga of the hostage crisis and the Soviet invasion of Afghanistan, the other big story of the day was Kennedy's campaign. Here was a living legend fixing to give the President a run for his money on his own turf. When, for instance, my former boss pulled out of a televised debate with the senator from Massachusetts, the Brits wanted my views on that, too. Who was really in charge at the White House? I was second-guessing, but so what? I'm rather proud of the phrase I coined about the President at this time. I said he was 'the hero of his own disasters', a line that was later used without attribution by Gerald Ford.

Every evening I would switch on the answering machine, lock up the office and take the one-five-nine back to St John's

Wood. If Ruth was out of town, I would cook myself a lonely supper, watch television or write to the kids, and go to bed early. I was drinking on my own for the first time in my life and hating myself for it.

When Ruth was around, I would seize the opportunity to go over to her place in Notting Hill Gate, and we would open a bottle of wine and fool around in bed. If, in a moment of euphoria, I spoke of buying a larger place for the two of us, she would invariably defer the decision. She would say we should discuss this 'once your business is up and running' or 'when interest rates are lower'.

The difficulty between us, I now realise, was that I was the one who had made the sacrifice. I had crossed the Atlantic, left the world I knew behind and taken a gamble. In return I expected a commitment that, temperamentally, she could not give. She had said: 'Trust yourself for a change.' And I had. My determination to rise to her challenge scared her a little, I think. After I had made my decision, she would say: 'Are you sure you want to do this?', and at first I imagined she was thoughtfully protecting me from disappointment and anticlimax. Then I saw that she was protecting her own independence. Once I landed in England, our relationship was under sentence.

I discovered that Ruth was not ready for what I was offering. Perhaps she never would be ready. In my fantasy, she was Beatrice to my Benedick, but I was coming to terms with the idea that we were not acting in the same play. I was ready to relax and have a good time, but she found and expressed herself through her work. She had few, if any, real friends. She knew everyone, and no one.

I was always amazed during the months that we were together how many tight-knit London circles she had penetrated. We would go to houses in Kensington, Chelsea and Holland Park, to families so white, so British and so established, you would have thought you would need a blood test to cross the threshold. Yet here was Ruth calling the lady of the house by her pet name, teasing her host as though she had known him for years, telling outrageous jokes – and getting away with it!

At home, there was less laughter. The flip side of the Australian banter was Ruth's sense of injustice and her determination to escape what she saw as the corruption of the old country. They say that when actors want to simulate grief, they laugh. There was something hysterical about Ruth's joy. She had joked to my father about the chains on her ankles, but I knew from experience that, psychologically speaking, their painful mark was still on her flesh.

I said I was a Gilchrist, but she treated me as a Lefevre. I would remonstrate with her, and say there was nothing worse than being the son of a father you felt obliged to betray.

'At least he doesn't deny your existence,' she said.

'Sometimes,' I replied, 'I wish he would. It might be easier then.'

'I don't understand you,' she said. 'He's a lovely guy, a real dad. If I was you I'd be proud of him.'

'You don't understand,' I said, unconsciously echoing her words.

Now, when I recall this conversation, I realise that I should have challenged her enthusiasm for my father, and inquired more deeply. At the time, I'm afraid I was not listening properly and didn't hear what she was saying.

12

The inquest into the untimely death of Jeffrey Roberts, bookseller, was finally convened before the coroner at Dorchester's County Hall in the last week of January.

Across the Atlantic, in the *Herald Tribune*, from my home town, came the obituaries for William O. Douglas, the longest-serving judge on the Supreme Court. A colourful, hard-living character, he had known my grandfather, and the news made me homesick for Washington. Elsewhere, the world was going crazy. Gold was eight hundred and something dollars an ounce. On the White House grapevine, I heard that the President was going to ask for more military spending in his State of the Union address. The Cold War, it seemed, was back with a vengeance. Perhaps I was right, after all, to be away from DC.

The streets of Dorchester are dark and narrow, with many bloody associations. Over the centuries, the local assizes have sent hundreds, even thousands, to Botany Bay or the gallows, as Ruth was not slow to remind me. When we arrived outside the County Hall there were quite a few people, a TV crew, one or two reporters, half a dozen cops and the usual throng of ghoulish onlookers. I noted with shock that everyone seemed to take it for granted that this mundane, municipal occasion was only the curtain-raiser to a larger, more sombre, drama.

I could see no sign of Marshall. Ruth was eager to get inside and secure a seat. At the last minute, I changed my mind. Sure, I was curious to see British justice at work, but there was something voyeuristic and distasteful about our presence. What would I say to Marshall if I met him? Good luck, old chap? I touched Ruth on the arm, and said I would see her at lunchtime. I hurried away to the car before she could protest.

I sat behind the wheel of the VW and stared through the foggy windscreen. I had no idea where to go or what to do. I picked up the road map from the passenger seat. Just outside the town was an ancient monument, Maiden Castle. I'd only a dim recollection of aerial photographs in a school book, but at least it offered a destination and a raison d'être. A few minutes later I pushed through the rusty gate and found myself on the perimeter of an Iron Age fort, massive grassy earthworks rearing in front of me like the flanks of some prehistoric beast.

I strolled through a gap in the fortifications. The morning sun shone like a light bulb through the winter mist. The phrase 'Keep up your bright swords, for the dew will rust them' came into my head. I scrambled up one of the ramparts, slipping and sliding in my city shoes. My hands became muddy with wormcasts. At the top I found a view of Wessex.

It was odd to imagine people living here one, even two, thousand years before, men and women like Ruth and myself, with loves and fears and hatreds, living and dying and worrying about tomorrow. At that precise moment, I felt extraordinarily in touch with the earth and my place on it. I felt as though insignificance meant something, after all, that something was passed on, from generation to generation. My anxieties receded. Whatever would happen would happen, and there was nothing I could do about it. I went and sat on a bench, placed in memory of some local bigwig.

As I was sitting there, a figure materialised out of the mist, a young man with a knapsack, a solitary tourist.

'Hi,' I said, recognising an American abroad.

'Oh, hi.' He paused, checking me out. 'Where are you from?'

I hesitated. I could have been confusing and gone British

97

on him, but to what purpose? 'I was raised on the East coast,' I said, 'but right now I'm living here.'

'Like it?'

I nodded. 'It's okay.'

He squared his shoulders and addressed me as though he had not spoken for days. 'I'm taking the plane to Chicago Friday, and I'm telling you it can't happen soon enough. This place sucks. No one understands a word I say, nothing works, and everything costs twice as much as it does at home. My folks said I'd have a real nice vacation, but hell, I reckon I'd have a better time in Tehran . . .'

There was more in the same vein but I forget it. Finally, the young man stopped. 'Nice talking to you,' he said, suddenly mild again. He gave a little military salute. 'See you later.' He seemed quite forlorn as he drifted away into the mist.

I have no idea how long I sat there, alone with my thoughts, but in due course I became aware of the cold and walked back to the car.

As I came down the hill into Dorchester, I passed a pay phone. On impulse I decided to call my father, and pulled over. It was one of those old-fashioned British telephone booths where you dialled the number and when the pips started you pushed in the money.

I dialled the number. Almost at once I heard my father's voice. 'Hello . . . hello . . .'

Pip-pip-pip.

But I could not speak to him. I slammed the receiver down and pushed the door open in a fluster. There was a punk waiting outside, a young punk with big breasts, bleached, spiky hair, torn jeans and a coat embroidered with swastikas. She was, inevitably, wearing safety-pins in her ears. Her death's-head make-up accentuated the smallness of her features.

'Spare some change?'

For some reason, I found myself sympathising with

my disenchanted fellow American. Why should I give these people money? I shook my head and hurried back to the car. She came after me. 'Go on. Lend us a quid, mister.'

I feared she would ask for a lift and found myself almost running.

'What's the matter with you?' The punk was enjoying herself. 'Do I scare you?'

I slammed the door and started the engine. She pressed her face to the window. Her voice was muffled, as if underwater. 'Go and fuck yourself, you tight-fisted bastard.'

Ruth was waiting outside the court. She began to describe the events of the morning. The coroner was deaf. The police were bent. The pathologist was a dud. Things were looking as bad as they could do.

I did not know how to respond or what to say. Perhaps Marshall was right. Perhaps he was done for.

In the High Street, we found a pub for lunch. Ruth identified two or three court officials for my benefit. Marshall, apparently, had headed off with his wife, alone. 'She looks like a good stick,' Ruth observed. She began to goad me for my failure to attend. 'Marshall needs all the support he can get, especially from you. When he saw me at the back of the court he looked so chuffed.' She seemed frustrated by my detachment. 'Is there nothing you can do for him?'

Suddenly, an idea that had been taking shape all morning came spontaneously to my lips. I said: 'I've decided to go to Northern Ireland for a few days. I have to see what his story adds up to for myself.'

'I just don't understand you, Sam.'

I was gratified by her amazement. I had taken the wind out of her sails. I was glad that, for once, I was doing the leaving. 'If things seem so black for Marshall, don't you think someone should do him the favour of looking into the background?' I explained that I still had my notes from our first meeting in seventy-seven. 'I don't think anyone has ever really bothered to investigate what he's been saying.'

'No one,' she replied, 'has been sitting on such good material.' There was bitterness in her voice. 'You've obviously forgotten how angry you were that time I was in Belfast.'

Nothing she could say could touch me. I was on my way.

We agreed that she would stay to give Marshall moral support. I would go at once to Belfast. She would, after all, give me some guidance. We would get in touch at the end of the week and compare notes. She would not let on where I was.

After lunch we strolled through the town and came to a brown river. There was a muddy towpath running past some willows but we did not take it.

'Look,' said Ruth. 'A kissing-gate.'

I took her in my arms and we kissed.

'Will you miss me?'

'If you stay away too long,' she replied. Then she laughed and looked away. 'If I get bored I could always drive over and visit your dad.'

'Sure,' I said. 'I expect he'd like that.'

She smiled and looked away. 'Promise I won't upset him.'

I slipped out of her embrace, hardly hearing her words. 'I must go if I'm going,' I said. 'I should find the nearest train station.'

Privately, I was eager to get away. I wanted to be on my own. I wanted to check into a large, anonymous hotel and try to make sense of Marshall's story in the place where it had occurred. I would do what perhaps I should have done three summers ago. I would take him seriously.

It is my misfortune that what I would find should take a further three years to bring to the page. But that is because while my father was alive I found it hard to express my discovery for myself, in words I could put my name to. It was only once he died that I felt able to speak for myself, perhaps because it was only after he was scattered to the four winds that I could begin to contemplate what he had done to me.

13

I left my car with Ruth and caught the slow train back to London. I did not mind our stop-start progress across southern England. My imagination was turning over the possibilities of the unknown. I had crossed my private Rubicon. I had made the decision to investigate Marshall's story. I was on my way.

I went straight to my office. Rosemary, who seemed, to my half-English eye, to have stepped from the pages of a Laura Ashley catalogue, was reading *Vogue* and eating a sticky bun. I could hardly complain. Her desk was empty. I announced that I was going abroad for a week on a business trip. I would phone in for messages. I wanted to sound like a busy executive, but I expect I gave the impression of a swindler on the lam.

It was getting late when I reached North London. Mr Upjohn's premises seemed more than usually cheerless. I was glad to be leaving. I threw some things into a bag and ordered a taxi for the morning, arguing with myself about the expense. Then I went to bed and sat up with the notes I had made after my encounter with Marshall in the summer of seventy-seven, half a dozen pages of scribble scattered with dates and telephone numbers.

Next day I took the first shuttle to Belfast. The cloud was low, and a blustery wet wind buffeted the passengers arriving at the terminal. Our plane lifted through the grey into the clear blue morning moments after take-off. My eyes hurt in the sudden sunshine, but my spirits were rising. I was like a prisoner released from a long captivity. As we levelled off I opened my briefcase and went over my notes once more. For the first time since arriving in England, I had found a purpose.

To my great regret, I had never been to Belfast, though I had seen the place often enough on the television. For many Americans it seems as remote and dangerous as the Wild West, but in truth it's probably as risky to take a walk down the Lower East Side. Like most foreign visitors, I had made a reservation at the Europa Hotel.

I checked in. There were security guards on the door, and the foyer was scuffed and poorly lit, but the staff were welcoming, as if to compensate for the threat of violence. My room was functional, with a glimpse of the domes of City Hall. Besides a hard-looking bed, there was a small television, a half-empty minibar, a telephone and a cubbyhole bathroom. It was all I needed.

I sat on the bed and pondered my first move. Marshall had mentioned the name of Jimmy Stewart several times during our conversation. Stewart was a journalist, a broadcaster with the BBC, and a good friend. I had both his home and office numbers.

I took a deep breath and picked up the phone.

I soon discovered that 'wee Jimmy' was not at home and not in his office. The idea that he could be found at either was, apparently, almost preposterous. The chances were that he would be at his favourite pub, the Crown, just across the road.

I went out. Belfast is battleship-grey, a northern pile of a place with granite municipal buildings. You don't have to look hard for the Troubles. There are Land-Rovers and armoured cars scattered through the traffic. The soldiers on foot patrol wear flak jackets and carry automatic weapons. In the city streets there's a general air of watchfulness. Americans like to joke that Britain is part of the Third World, but when you see troops standing in the doorways of supermarkets, the joke seems a little near the bone.

I went across to the Crown in a matter of minutes and stepped inside. The cosy Victorian interior was also familiar from television documentaries. The bartender directed me to a little booth at the far end of the saloon. Stewart was sitting alone, making notes in the margin of a script.

I introduced myself.

He was a small man with a thatch of squirrel-grey hair and the brick-red cheeks of a drinker. I saw his wary, calculating look and offered him a pint, though he was not halfway through the one he had to hand. He accepted. He seemed quite matter-of-fact about the interruption, as though he was used to public recognition.

It was not until I sat down opposite, with Guinness for both of us, that he showed any curiosity towards my intrusion. 'So now tell me, Mr Gilchrist, what brings you to Belfast?'

'Your friend Craig Marshall,' I said.

He picked up the newspaper beside him with studied casualness, but I could see his attention was focused. 'There's a piece in today's paper about that case,' he said, turning the pages. 'Would he be a friend of yours?'

I nodded, not wanting to elaborate. 'I gather you knew each other in the old days.'

' "The old days"?' Stewart played with my words. 'I reckon they are "the old days" now. Five years is a long time in a place like this.'

'You've lived here all your life, I suppose.'

'You suppose right, young man. Tell me, now, what part of the United States are you from?'

'Washington, DC.'

'Dodge City.' He smiled to himself. 'I never was there, but I visited New York – Noo Yawk – once. A fine, mad city.'

'Perhaps you could say the same about Belfast.'

Stewart shook his head. 'This is not a city. This is several tribal villages fighting among themselves. A great city has to have the world passing through it. No one passes through Belfast, not if they can help it.' He laughed and sipped his drink. 'Tell me, how is the poor old major?'

'Surviving.'

'He always was a survivor.' He gestured at the newspaper. 'What really happened?'

'I don't know.' I paused. 'That's why I've come to see you.'

Stewart frowned and gave me that wary look. 'Are you a newspaper man, Mr Gilchrist?'

I explained the circumstances of my first meeting with Marshall. 'Frankly, I was sceptical. Now, for various reasons, I am starting to revise my opinions.' I introduced a note of flattery. 'Marshall said that if there was one man who had the full story it was you.'

Stewart shook his head. 'I doubt there is a full story.'

I wondered if I could needle a response out of him. 'Perhaps, like me, you chose to do nothing with what you knew.'

The colour blazed in his cheeks. 'Good journalists always have half a dozen leads they haven't the time to follow up.' He took another sip of Guinness, and became calmer. 'If you lived here, young man, you might learn to adopt a less crusading attitude to life.'

I found it exhilarating to hear myself described in such unfamiliar terms. 'I'm not crusading,' I replied. 'I've just become a little curious about Marshall's claims.'

Stewart looked at me with suspicion, as if he was personally implicated. 'And what would they be?'

'He says he was framed.'

Stewart seemed to find my vocabulary entertaining. 'They've been framing him, as you put it, for years. There are more frames round Major Craig Marshall than there are in a roomful of Rembrandts.'

'So what's he taking the fall for?'

'Mr Gilchrist.' Stewart yawned and stretched his arms. 'You are obviously an excitable young American who has been reading too much Raymond Chandler. This is not Los Angeles and I am not Humphrey Bogart. This is a war zone. People do terrible things in wars, and this one is no

105

exception. Marshall was part of that war. He got caught in no-man's-land when someone happened to send up a flare. There are, I'm afraid, dozens like him. Good people who find themselves in the wrong place at the wrong time.'

I was silenced by his cynicism.

'Look,' he continued, 'Marshall is a decent man, too decent for his own good, probably. When he joined the Army, it was a good ticket. A house and a uniform, a bit of square-bashing and some nice trips to the sunny parts of the world to keep the natives in order. But then this place goes up in smoke. This is different.'

'He told me,' I said, remembering my notes, 'that he fell in love with Northern Ireland.'

'The Scots often do. It reminds them of home.'

'He was a public relations officer, I believe.'

'That was his title. On paper, it meant he was assigned to VIP visitors, politicians on fact-finding missions and businessmen worrying about their investments. His job was to put the military's point of view in the best possible light. As the crisis developed, he found himself in charge of something much closer to Army propaganda.'

'Was he good at that?'

'How well would you say you knew him?'

'We've met a few times. Not well, I suppose.'

'He was brilliant. You've probably seen his Walter Mitty side, his capacity to believe his own fantasies. He would spin stories for the press that were little short of genius.'

I remembered Marshall telling me that everyone went slightly crazy over here. 'But something made him panic,' I said.

'He was encouraged by his superiors to take risks and he got carried away by what he was doing. Then he discovered he had gone too far down a certain path. He was off the map, out in no-man's-land. That's when the flare went up.'

I wanted to press for an explanation, but something told

106

me to be patient. 'If you put it like that,' I said, 'you could say he's still shell-shocked.'

'A situation like this attracts all sorts of funny characters. You've got psychopaths calling themselves freedom fighters, torturers who claim to be interrogators, bullyboys masquerading as policemen. It's a strange little laboratory of the human spirit we have built for ourselves, Mr Gilchrist, and not many people know about it. Marshall's mistake was to confuse his fantasies with reality.'

I said: 'The miracle is that people manage any kind of normal life at all.'

'Normality is a surprisingly tenacious quality that surfaces in the most unusual situations. Only then people call it banality.'

'There's a lot to be said for banality,' I said.

Stewart laughed at this and I felt, at that moment, as though I was still in with a chance.

Now it was his turn to exercise his curiosity, and I let him. I had time on my side. 'Washington, DC,' he said. 'Tell me, what kind of life do you have there?'

I explained my circumstances as well as I could. There was no advantage to be gained from holding back.

Stewart listened. As I told my tale, I felt I was becoming, in his eyes, a more interesting person. 'Well,' he remarked, as I drew to a close. 'They say it's love that makes the world go round.' He paused to finish his drink. 'Love and money.' He looked sadly into his empty glass. 'Two things I could do with at the moment.' He looked at me frankly. 'You'll have a hard time tracing Marshall's story now. Most of the people from that time have gone, one way or another.'

It was the moment to make my appeal. I had no choice. 'Would you help me – for the sake of the old days?'

He gave a casual, dismissive burp. I could see he did not like to be put on the spot. 'I'll see what I can do, but don't count on it.' He was gathering up his papers. 'If you'll excuse me, Mr Gilchrist, I have a broadcast to make.' When he stood up he was slightly bow-legged, like a jockey. 'Where are you staying?'

'The Europa.'

'Give my regards to the major when you speak to him.'

'I don't think you understand,' I said. 'He has no idea I'm here. I'm a free agent.'

'In this place,' he answered, giving me a strange look, 'no one is a free agent.'

At the time, I thought he was speaking for effect. Now, I'm not so sure.

14

A day passed, and then another. I read the newspapers. Everyone was debating the Old Man's chances of re-election. I ordered room service, thin sandwiches and stewed, British coffee. I found a bookstore and bought a bagful of paperbacks. I was not adventurous, but if I went out, I always checked at the desk on my return. There were no messages. I decided 'Wee Jimmy' was testing me. It would be a mistake to phone him. I lay on my narrow bed with a copy of *Under Western Eyes*, and waited.

Ruth rang. 'Bad news,' she said. 'The coroner decided that it was an unlawful killing by a person or persons unknown.'

'Where's Marshall?'

'He went home with his wife. He's still just a witness.'

'What are the police playing at?'

'The usual game of cat-and-mouse. They pulled him in for more questioning, then let him go. He says it's only a matter of time before they arrest him. Isn't there anything you can do?'

I explained I was making slow progress. 'Did you visit my father?'

'Don't be silly.' Her laugh was quick to fill the gap. 'I wasn't being serious.'

'Where are you now?'

'I'm in bed,' she replied. 'Why don't you make love to me?'

But my fantasy unit was on the blink. I wondered who else might be sharing this call. 'Phonus interruptus, I'm afraid.' I did my telephone laugh. 'I'll call you tomorrow.'

I lay in the dark pondering Marshall's future. Everyone, even Ruth, seemed so resigned to his fate. That was the worst of England, the oppressive sense of historical prede-termination.

I was asleep when the phone rang again. I recognised Stewart's voice at once. He would be waiting outside for me at nine o'clock.

Stewart's car was in better condition than its owner. He drove it at a stately thirty, as if taking a rare model to a vintage rally. He was dressed for a day at the races – sport coat, tartan scarf and pork-pie hat. As he drove, he pointed out the landmarks, the Falls Road and the Shankill, Harland and Wolff, the Milltown cemetery and so on. From time to time he would light up a Hamlet cigar. As we left the city and reached the freeway, Stewart said: 'We're going to Armagh. There's a fellow there by the name of Bob McCartney who'll be glad to meet you.'

I remembered McCartney's name from my notes and recalled that he had been Marshall's driver.

On the open road, Stewart took the car up to a death-defying fifty and in due course we came cruising into the town of Armagh. 'We'll skip the sights,' he said. 'Bob lives in a nice little village just outside.'

In a couple of miles we were passing through apple orchards, heading towards the border. This, I knew from my research, was the part of the province the newspapers call 'bandit country'.

The village was a backwater, a hundred yards off the main road, as though life itself was passing it by. Stewart negotiated the anti-terrorist bollards and turned into an emp-ty square with a war memorial. Beyond, a row of red-brick Victorian working men's houses was arranged into a single main street. In the near distance, there was a mill chimney, a stern reminder of a forgotten regime.

'Bob's lived here all his life,' said Stewart, parking the car. 'His father was a foreman at the mill. That's all gone now, of course.'

McCartney was on the doorstep to greet us. He was

a large, roly-poly man in a knitted waistcoat and slippers. He might have been a retired publican. His handshake was warm and soft and we were hardly through the door before he was offering a glass of whisky 'to take the chill off the morning'.

The crowded parlour was a museum of McCartney family history: seaside photographs, framed citations and commemorative plates. There was a bronze model of the Empire State Building by the television and a collection of souvenir paperweights on the mantelshelf. Among the clutter on the sideboard opposite the fireplace, I spotted an old wooden flute. McCartney caught me looking at it, as he came in with the drinks.

'There's quite a tale goes with that flute. The boy that had it was my father's best friend. He was killed on the Somme and my father, who was with him when he fell, saved it and brought it home. It still makes a lovely sound.' He picked it up and began to play the National Anthem. After a few quavering bars he stopped. 'Tell me, Mr Gilchrist, how is Major Marshall?'

'I expect you've seen the press coverage,' I replied.

'Who could ever believe the newspapers?' observed McCartney. 'How is he in himself?'

'You know how tough he is,' I said.

My answer seemed to bring back memories. 'I've seen him do eighteen, even twenty hours at a stretch, have a kip in the clothes he was standing up in, and then carry on again, sometimes for days on end.' He tasted his whisky like a connoisseur. 'I've seen him up, and I've seen him down. I've seen him in his parade ground number ones and I've seen him covered in muck and mire after a surveillance exercise. I was the squire to his knight, if you like, Mr Gilchrist, and proud to be so.'

'He was a good soldier,' Stewart remarked.

McCartney looked at me from his fireside. 'Tell me, Mr Gilchrist, how did you come to meet the major?'

I explained.

Stewart smiled. 'There's always a girl in it somewhere,' he said, as if confirming a universal law.

McCartney shook his head at his friend. 'The major was attractive to women,' he said, 'but whatever the newspaper boys want to say, he was faithful to his wife in his heart. I'm sure of that. I worked for him all the time he was here. There's nothing I don't know about the major.'

This was my chance and I took it. 'Will you tell me what happened?'

McCartney looked at Stewart, who nodded. Presumably I had been checked out. I wondered vaguely how much they knew about me.

'It didn't happen overnight,' he began. 'Things only began to get out of hand once the mainland got involved.' He paused for a moment. 'Did you Americans ever see a television series by the name of Monty Python's Flying Circus?'

'Sure,' I said, with a smile. 'Know what I mean, nudge nudge, snap snap, grin grin, wink wink, say no more.'

McCartney was smiling too. 'My favourite was the lumberjack song.' He became serious. 'No matter,' he went on. 'Did the major ever mention Operation Monty Python?'

I had held myself back for long enough. It was time to come out into the open. 'He spoke about it when we first met. I'm afraid I couldn't, or wouldn't, believe him.'

There was a long silence. I heard a clock ticking in the hallway.

McCartney stirred in his chair. 'Then what are you doing here?' There was puzzlement in his voice, not hostility.

'You could say I've changed my mind,' I confessed.

McCartney nodded, as if he too had once had doubts. 'I remember the first time I heard about it, I was shocked. The major was worried. He said to me: "Bob, I'm being asked to do things I don't like. They say that if I'm not with them, I'm against them. They've asked me –" ' McCartney stopped. 'What you have to understand, Mr Gilchrist, is that everyone trusted the major. The officials, the men, the press boys, everyone. They believed what he said, even when he was telling lies.'

Perhaps, I thought, this explained why Marshall disliked my persistent scepticism. He was used to conning people.

'Propaganda, Mr Gilchrist, that was his skill. So of course these people wanted him on their side. But, believe me, he didn't like it.'

'So he did resign?'

'Oh yes,' said McCartney quickly. 'He resigned all right. He told me he'd had enough. His wife was afraid, he said, and he wanted to get out while he was still young enough to get another job.'

'It wasn't easy,' I said. 'He claims that once he left his masters went out of their way to stop him.'

'Does he indeed?' said Stewart, speaking quietly.

'There were some powerful people behind the operation,' said McCartney. He was on his feet with the bottle. 'Will you take the other half now, Mr Gilchrist?'

'Thank you.'

He filled our glasses and sat back. Outside, in the street, children's voices twittered in the cold.

'What sort of powerful people?' I wondered.

McCartney stared into his glass. 'It's hard to say who were the biggest troublemakers. At the beginning, there were the real hotheads, the young turks. They first had the idea for the operation. The senior men on the mainland were swept into it by the young turks after one too many at the nineteenth hole. They probably regret it now.'

'How many were involved, would you say?'

'I don't think the major was ever sure. Perhaps thirty. When you look back at it now, it seems crazy. At the time, with all the talk, it seemed to make more sense.'

'What talk?'

113

'Oh, you know, the crisis in government and the Lord knows what.' He tipped his glass. 'As you can see, Mr Gilchrist, I'm not a political man myself.'

They say that good interrogators should always ask the question to which they already know the answer to elicit the missing detail that will clinch the case. In my heart I knew the answer to my next question, but I had to have McCartney confirm it.

'Who were these senior men?' I asked. 'Did the major mention names?'

'There weren't many.' He was thinking aloud. 'There was a fellow named Harris, code-name Bomber. There was a fellow I never saw, code-name Judas. And there was an ex-naval man, Lefevre, code-name Eagle.'

I tried to sound casual. 'What was Lefevre doing over here?'

'No idea.' McCartney shook his head. 'He wasn't your usual ministry type. He and the major used to play squash together.'

'What happened to the operation?'

'I lost my job, so I don't know the details, but I have the sense of the situation. After the major left, the whole exercise was put on the back burner.'

'It was wound up, I heard,' said Stewart, chipping in.

'There was a big reshuffle. The Army had gone too far, and there were rival services waiting to get even. The young turks were redeployed, God knows where, and everyone went back to hunting terrorists. No doubt the generals continued to grumble away in their clubs and write letters to *The Times*.'

'Perhaps Marshall is right,' I said. 'Perhaps the men from the ministry did go after him.'

'It wouldn't be the first time that's happened here,' Stewart commented. He seemed to know what he was talking about.

'Could it have worked?' I asked. 'Could Monty Python have happened?'

Stewart looked at me with amusement. 'But it has worked.'

'I don't understand.'

'Think about it, Mr Gilchrist. These men were afraid that unless they did something drastic the ship of state would run on the rocks. They wanted strong leadership, what they called a national government. You're a political fellow. Wouldn't you agree that this country now has the most authoritarian prime minister in living memory?'

I could not stop my instinctive, democratic response. 'You're forgetting that it was elected.'

'But the electorate had no choice, Mr Gilchrist. Look around at the alternatives.' Stewart paused. 'All discredited.'

McCartney spoke out of the shadows by the fire. 'And guess who discredited them?'

I shook my head.

'The smiling snake,' Stewart replied. 'Our old friend Monty Python.'

'Now you see,' said McCartney, 'why they might want to make sure that no one believed Major Marshall's story.'

He picked up the old flute and trilled a few bars of Rule Britannia. Then, apparently on impulse, he handed it to me.

'There you are,' he said. 'Give it to the major for me, would you? A tribute from one fallen comrade to another.'

15

The light was almost gone when Stewart returned me to the Europa. I had eaten nothing all day and was quite drunk, so drunk, as the hillbillies say, I couldn't hit the wall with a handful of beans. McCartney seemed to live on whisky. Stewart's cheeks were flaming, but he was still in control. I was grateful for his stately thirty. We said goodbye and I thanked him. He pressed me to call if I ever returned, but I knew we would not meet again. I could not imagine what would bring me back to Belfast. He was right. The city is part of no one's Grand Tour.

Alone in my room I lay down and slept deep and dreamlessly. When I woke, the message light was flashing on the bedside telephone. I called the front desk. 'A Miss Ritchie, sir.' She had left no number. I assumed she was back in London. But I did not return her call. I lacked the resolution. I was not a happy camper. Where would I ever begin?

My head was pounding. I swallowed four aspirin, and washed them down with a Heineken from the minibar. After the companionship of the whisky I had enjoyed at McCartney's place, the beer seemed thin and inhospitable. I switched on the television and began channel-jumping. There was a soccer match in progress. I think it was Liverpool versus Sheffield Wednesday, but it doesn't matter. I wondered idly if there was a Sheffield Thursday or Friday. The game was a boring mudbath and I switched it off. I picked up the telephone again and asked for the operator. 'Is there by any chance a Sheffield Thursday?' 'Excuse me, sir?' 'I want to make an international call,' I said, sobering. I had the number by heart.

I heard the call connecting across the Atlantic. I saw my

house, and my wife helping Alice with her homework on the kitchen table. On the fourth ring she picked it up.

'Hi,' I said. There was a slight echo on the line. 'It's me.'

There was a long pause.

'What do you want?' she replied coldly. 'Where are you, Seymour?'

Apart from Marshall, my ex-wife is the only other person who would recall the priest's baptismal blessing. Lizzie is five years my senior, a big age-gap when we met in grad school. Almost from our first date, she treated me as a difficult child. What began as a kind of game ended up as the mannerism of emotional distance.

'I'm in Belfast.'

'What on earth are you doing there?'

'I don't really know. I thought I did, but now I don't.' I wanted help and I realised that she could not give it. There was so much of my life she knew nothing about. 'Do you remember the Monty Python show?'

'Are you drunk?'

'Not really. Look,' I said, 'I'm sorry.' There was another pause and 'sorry' echoed accusingly down the line. 'I wish I hadn't come here,' I added.

'I expect you wish a lot of things.'

I wish you were here, I thought to myself, you and Charlie and Alice. 'I've been talking to some people who knew my father in the good old days, I mean the bad old days, but that's not why I rang. We should talk,' I said. 'We should talk things over. It might help.'

'There's nothing more to say,' she replied at last. 'I'm going to ring off now. Please don't do this again.'

'Please – Lizzie – wait –'

There was a click and then the humming of the receiver in my hand. I lay back on the bed and felt the tears on my cheeks. But I was not crying for my wife, or even my children. These were tears of self-pity. I was on the

117

edge of the abyss. Once I was back in London I would have to confront the fact that Ruth and I were in trouble, too.

16

I flew to London next day with a hangover and arrived at
work towards the end of the morning. If you wanted to do
business with The Special Relationship you would have to
whistle for it. The stairwell was dark, the place closed up. I
unlocked and pushed open the door. Bills and advertisements
were strewn across the mat. On the desk in the room beyond
what I termed 'the front office', Hollywood-style, was an
envelope addressed to Seymour Gillchrist (*sic*) in round blue
handwriting. Rosemary had spoken to Mummy and Daddy
and they had advised her to quit, or, as she put it, in that
quaint English phrase, to hand in her notice.

As I sat there, my luggage on the floor, unopened bills
in front of me, my new business failing before my eyes,
the telephone rang.

I was about to impersonate the ideal assistant when the
answering machine clicked into action. It was my father.
He was coming up to London in a few days. Jane was
driving him. He would be staying at the club. Was there
any chance of a drink one evening? He suggested a time.
As usual, he offered no room for manoeuvre. Unless he
heard to the contrary, and the contrary was never part of
my father's expectations, he would await me there at the
appointed hour.

When I heard my father speaking the language of clubs
and cocktails I thought to myself that the James Bond of
boyhood make-believe was not so wide of the mark. The
Beaver inhabited a world as remote from real life as it was
possible to find. This was his choice and his destiny. Like
many Englishmen of his class and generation, he found the
society in which he was living a poor substitute for the society

of his youth, a world as extinct today as steam engines and magic lanterns.

The Beaver was a man whose life was behind him and now, as I stared at Rosemary's letter, I wondered if I was not about to follow in his footsteps. I had designed the letterhead myself. Perhaps Mummy and Daddy were right. If there was a Special Relationship it certainly wasn't happening here. Probably it wasn't happening anywhere. To employ another curious English formula, I was about to make myself 'redundant'.

I played my messages and opened my mail in a mood of desperation. Perhaps I would find the commission that would get me out of the hole, the invitation to represent one of the score of major corporations to whom I had posted my egregious mail shot. But I could not shake off my past. In America, the Republicans had accused the President of breaking no less than two hundred and twenty-seven campaign promises. Frankly, I didn't know we'd made that many, but it was clever tactics to go gunning for his honesty, his Achilles' heel. Once again I was being asked to provide a pithy comment for the newspapers.

Perhaps I should become a journalist and join the rat-pack in Fleet Street? No thank you. I had met several British press types in Ruth's company and a shabbier, more drunken bunch of good-for-nothings and sleazeballs it was hard to imagine. I would rather go home, my tail between my legs, than sink to that.

Home. Where was my home? I like to think I am equally at ease on both sides of the Atlantic, familiar with both worlds, but the unpalatable truth was that when I ceased to be a Lefevre and became a Gilchrist I began inexorably to lose touch with my British self. Just because I had learned to leave my accent, like unwanted contraband, outside the airport customs, I was in truth no less of 'a Yank'. If you cannot serve two masters, equally you cannot fly two flags. Given a choice between John Bull and Uncle Sam I would always square up behind my namesake.

It was at this moment that I resolved to act on this realisation. I had reached a crossroads. I would have that once-for-all conversation with Ruth we had both, in our different ways, evaded. Apart from my painful obligation to visit Marshall, what really mattered to me then was to discover the truth about Ruth's feelings towards me. If, after all, we had a future together, then I would give myself a second chance here, sell my services as a copywriter, buy a house perhaps, and make a go of things. If not, then I was still my own boss. I could return to America and pick up where I had left off, at least professionally speaking. Politics in Washington is a revolving door. There's always something to do, some kind of hack work to be found. Perhaps even my marriage was not irretrievably lost. At that point, in the early spring of 1980, I still had a certain self-confidence, an unmistakable personal zip. The worst was yet to come.

17

I should have remembered that, in the emotional transactions of men and women, there rarely is a definitive occasion. In retrospect, it was ridiculous to imagine, especially with one as elusive as Ruth, that we could achieve a decisive resolution of the uncertainties between us. You cannot hold a board meeting of the heart.

We arranged to meet in a quiet restaurant of Ruth's choice down in Fulham, one of the many that were springing up all over London at that time. The word 'yuppy' was just coming into circulation, and that was the atmosphere of the place. Most of the tables were occupied by slick young men in suits and stripey shirts entertaining smartly dressed women with perfect winter suntans.

She greeted me with her habitual 'Hello, darling', and a kiss, but I sensed there was something missing, a small space between herself and the expression of feeling. At the time I put it down to a preoccupation with her work, the inevitable deadline pressure, and anyway the moment passed. Once she was seated opposite, after more gallantry from the maître d', she seemed happy to be here, and glad to see me again.

'It seems ages,' she said with a smile.

'A lot of blood has flowed under this particular bridge,' I said. I explained that I had decided to close my office. This seemed a good preliminary to the mutual assessment of our own special relationship.

Ruth's response was characteristically brisk. 'If it isn't working out, better to cut your losses. You're quite a resourceful, clever fellow. I'm sure there are other things you can do.' She raised her glass. 'Onwards and upwards.'

I was inclined to forget, while I was away from her, how unsentimental Ruth could be. 'So how have you been?' I asked, making conversation.

She avoided the question, fussing with the menu. 'Let's get this out of the way,' she said. 'The way they do things here is so . . . Thank you, Pierre.' She accepted the wine list like a duchess and selected an expensive burgundy.

When we had finished ordering Ruth was quick to ask me about the trip to Belfast. I summarised my adventures as succinctly as I could. 'At the end of the day,' I said, using a phrase popular with many of the people I had spoken to over there, 'what Marshall claims is true, so far as I can discover. There was a plot, much as he described it two years ago, and my father was part of it. Now I'm left wondering what to do next.'

I had imagined she might want to sound off indignantly about Marshall's plight, the imminent prosecution we both feared, and the help I might give him. So it was a surprise when she said, with an indulgent smile, 'Your father never could resist getting into trouble, could he?'

'You don't seem too concerned,' I said.

'What's the point? He's one of those people who get away with things.'

'Usually with women,' I said, instantly regretting, from the look on Ruth's face, the querulous note that was creeping into my conversation.

But then she laughed, and I sensed it was at me. 'He's just a very charming man. What else can I tell you?'

I looked at her with dismay. Everything she said sounded like an implicit critique. I felt my temper rising. 'Well, I for one am not going to let him get away with his famous charm,' I said. 'I want to confront him with what I know before –' I stopped.

'Before?'

'Before he does any more damage,' I said, vainly covering

123

up my slip. 'I'm going to tell him he cannot brush this stuff under the carpet as he used to.'

'Good luck.'

'Why so cynical?'

'Nothing you can say will touch him. That's the sort of man he is. It's horribly appealing.' She looked at me. 'Sometimes I wonder how you can be so different.'

'I sometimes wonder myself.'

The waiter removed our plates and, to the annoyance of the adjoining table, Ruth lit a cigarette. It was as though she was determined to have a row with someone. Eventually, after a predictable exchange of acrimony, we were offered a better table at the other end of the restaurant. Ruth adored the fuss. I was relieved when peace was restored. As we settled down again, she said: 'I think you were about to tell me that you want to go home.'

'I don't know what I want. I feel a bit like the President. I'm in too deep.' I took her hand. 'Do you love me?'

'I hate that question.' She frowned. 'I loved you for the confident way you handled power. Now you're on your own here it's different. You seem less exotic. I'm sorry.' She squeezed my fingers. 'I don't want to hurt you. I recognise you're vulnerable.' She smiled. 'Unlike your father.'

'What d'you mean?'

She withdrew her hand from mine. I sensed that she was choosing her words carefully. 'Just that he struck me as a man impervious to hurt.'

I think I was slightly appalled. 'Do you admire that?'

'It makes a change to find someone who can handle the inevitable treacheries of love.'

'Find?'

She waved her cigarette. 'Only a manner of speaking.' She seemed to be remembering something. 'I've always said that life's short, and then you die. He understands this.' She shrugged. 'That's all.'

124

'Are you sure you've not seen him again?' I said, hating myself for the question.

She shook her head. Something made her hesitate. 'No,' she said.

A small silence came between us. With my inner eye I saw my father leaning on his stick in pain. Then I said: 'I never see you now. Whenever we meet I always feel under pressure. We need time together. We should take a holiday, like in the old days.'

'You can never go back.'

'We could still have a holiday.'

'Where?'

It was shortly after this that we decided to go to Spain and follow the pilgrim's route to Santiago de Compostela.

18

I reached my father's club, the Athenaeum, deliberately late. I did not want to have to linger in the marble hallway, as I had done as a boy, pretending to read the stock market prices and cricket scores on the tickertape machine under the suspicious eye of the porter. Today, I was expected, recognised. I am ashamed to admit that in my expatriate heart I was gratified to be treated as an honoured guest. 'The Admiral is waiting for you, sir,' said the doorman, directing me upstairs.

My father was alone in the library, playing chess by himself. I have to say that he was looking more than usually dashing in a pearl-grey double-breasted suit and watered silk nightclub tie. His lease on life was getting pretty short, but he still managed to put on a good show.

'A mug's game,' he remarked, waving at the chair opposite with his stick. 'I tell myself I'm giving white the advantages, but somehow black always wins.' As he watched me settle myself in his company, he murmured in that way he had: 'Night's black agents to their preys do rouse, do rouse.'

I have inherited his penchant for quotations, but I usually ignore his own snatches and titbits. 'Is Jane with you?'

'I've parked her in the ladies' annexe. She sends her love.'

This was to be a lone shoot-out, man to man. There was a waiter hovering in the distance. My father signalled for his regular evening drink, gin Martini, automatically including me in his order. I knew better than to contradict his choice. Around us, on the walls, portraits of British imperial heroes looked down impassively.

I had dreamed of this place the night before. I was with Mother. She was dressed in black like a Victorian governess. In the middle of the room, flooded with light, was a bank of lilies, concealing an open coffin. 'Your father's dead,' my mother whispered. In the darkened alcoves of the library I heard friends and family repeat her words. 'My father's dead,' I said, and began to cry. I wanted to approach the casket, but I could not. All at once we were outside in a lumpy grass cemetery. The coffin was being lowered into the grave and I was standing next to my mother, throwing crumbly handfuls of earth after it.

I woke with tears on my cheeks. It was a few moments before I realised my father was not dead and that I had been dreaming. I must confess I was frightened by the dream and strangely grateful to have the Beaver, as large as life, in front of me now.

The drinks arrived and we toasted our respective healths, as though we were the oldest of old friends.

My father nodded at the chess board. 'Fancy a game?'

'I haven't played for ages.'

'A friendly.' He was already setting up the pieces. 'You can have white.'

'What brings you to London?' I asked, moving my king's pawn two squares.

'I had been hoping to take the train and have an amusing evening *à deux*,' he murmured, with a quite unnecessary confidentiality. 'But Jane in her wisdom decided I was not well enough to travel on my own. These days I'm afraid I have to let her have her way.' He met my pawn, mid-board. 'How are the mighty fallen!'

In the past, before his rendezvous with the emissaries from the undiscovered country, my father's idea of an amusing evening *à deux* was two bottles of good wine, an audience for his stories, some flirtatious chatter and, if he was lucky, what he called 'a bit of nookie'.

'Well, fings ain't what they used to be.' I moved my queen's knight into battle.

'Speaking of the fair sex, how is that rambunctious young lady of yours?'

I decided to test him. 'She didn't visit you?'

He looked at me steadily. 'Why on earth should she want to do that?' He moved another pawn into action.

'No reason, I suppose. But she was down your way and said she might.' I parried his attack. 'She really likes you,' I said.

'Ditto. Double ditto.' He tossed a pawn lightly in his hand. 'You're a lucky chap, Sam.' He smiled. 'But you'll have to keep an eye on her.'

'I do my best,' I said. 'But occasionally I have to be out of town.' I sighed. 'And so does she of course.'

'I understand.'

'In fact,' I said, moving the conversation nearer the target area, 'I was away this week.'

'So I realise.' He placed the advancing pawn on the board. 'I've tried to reach you several times.'

I opened up my king's bishop, wondering where this gambit would lead. I had resolved, in anticipation of our conversation, to be firm. 'I went to Belfast.'

I studied his face for a reaction, but he was concentrating on the game, and giving nothing away. 'A brave city,' he said, replying with a knight.

'I had quite a time.' I advanced another pawn. 'Some people remember you rather well.'

'I liked the North.' He was counter-attacking. 'The Irish really understand the meaning of the word hospitality.'

'There are still one or two who haven't forgotten Operation Monty Python,' I said, moving my bishop into the middle of the board.

I have to hand it to him. He didn't move a muscle. The Beaver was an old pro who had been in any number of tricky situations. He knew when the game was up and he always adapted, tactically, to new circumstances. If his troops were outnumbered, his retreat cut off and his ammunition exhausted, no one in the world would sue for peace with greater charm.

'It always amazes me,' he said, sitting back with his cocktail, 'how the Irish cherish their memories. They'll talk about something in their bars and parlours until it becomes part of the local legend. Like a great artist with an oil painting they'll work it over and over until the picture they give you is the picture they wanted you to see in the first place, though it may have nothing to do with the actual landscape.' His private smile suggested he was amused by my challenge. 'I'm sure that dear old Monty Python –' even his inflection cast doubt on the operation '– sounds far more convincing now than when it was the madcap scheme of a few excitable young men from the security services.'

'But –' I tried to interrupt. He was rewriting history before my very eyes. He anticipated my objections, putting up his hand.

'No, I'm not going to deny the past, and I won't take back anything we have said to each other before, but I want to suggest that you don't make the cardinal error of taking it too seriously.' He was impressively matter-of-fact. 'I, for one, saw the operation as a way of alerting some rather mediocre politicians to the gravity of the situation. It was high time they were reminded of their responsibilities. To me, it was only a bit of mischief.' He rubbed his hands together and made another move. 'Ah! mischief . . .'

'If it was only mischief, why is a man about to go on trial for a murder he did not commit?'

He had no trouble with this, either. As I listened, I decided I had to respect my father's capacity for steering through rough seas to calmer waters. He believed in luck and optimism and, for most of his life, his luck had held.

'You know something, Sam, I loved your mother for her American mind, and you've inherited it, that determination to see justice done and right prevail, regardless of the circumstances.'

He would not let me speak again, and I knew better

than to argue. Jane had advised me that his illness made him irrationally short-tempered.

'It's the one bit of idealism left in the States, this obsession with conspiracies. What a puritan lot you great capitalists are! Excuse me, Sam, but unless I have missed something, your Major Marshall is walking the streets a free man.'

'A free man who is waiting to be arrested.' I moved my second knight into action.

'Then perhaps he does have a case to answer.' He pondered his move. 'You can't deny that he lied to the police, Sam.'

'It was an honourable lie.'

My father shrugged. 'These are matters of interpretation, even of faith. The fact of the matter is that he is still very much at large.' He almost chuckled. 'You could say it was a triumph of British justice.'

He sounded so reasonable it seemed perverse to disagree, but I kept my resolve. 'Or a cock-up at the ministry. I imagine they're still fixing the evidence against him.'

How often as a teenager had I argued with him in this tone. I was an adult now, but still he was humouring me. 'You people have got Watergate fever and you have got it bad. It's extraordinary. The most powerful nation on earth and you don't trust a soul. You cannot accept the possibility of an event that occurs without some sinister twist.'

'Perhaps we are right not to.'

He ignored me, brooding on the game. 'The Chair she sat in, like a burnished throne, glowed on the marble . . . pom . . . pom . . . O O O O that Shakespeherian Rag, it's so elegant, so intelligent . . . pom . . . pom . . .'

We played several moves without speaking. I should never have given him black. He was advancing his pieces in a devastating pincer movement. A better player would have resigned. Finally he remarked: 'We have spoken before of these things. In retrospect, yes, I admit that it was ill-advised, but that's all downriver now. If there are people who are

130

pursuing the kind of vendetta against Marshall you suggest, then I am not advised of it. One hears things all the time, of course, but it's gossip. If I believed everything I had heard in this club I should –' he paused for effect. 'I should go and live in the Australian outback.' His little joke enabled him to change direction again. 'Odd that you and Marshall should have met. Do you have a conspiracy theory for that, too?'

We both laughed. He was an old rogue and he knew it. If you had walked in just then you would have seen father and son apparently in perfect accord.

'The conspiracy's name is Ruth Ritchie,' I replied.

'That girl gets everywhere,' he said neutrally.

'She and Marshall go back several years.'

'I see.' He digested this information while I contemplated my threatened annihilation. 'Well, I don't believe in advice, but if I may give a word to the wise, I'd leave well alone.'

So there was his message, the raison d'être of our meeting. I see now that he did not want his son caught up in Marshall's destruction. In his own funny way he was trying to do me some good, and himself of course. To this day, I have no idea if he was operating under instructions or merely acting off his own bat, as he would put it. All I know is that he repeated himself in the way I remembered from childhood, 'a word to the wise, leave well alone', and then, light and airy as a character from the Drones Club, disposed of my feeble defences in a few swift moves.

The moment for telling him of my business failure and my proposed departure, the moment for anything serious, slipped by. My father simply wanted to forget the past, bury its difficulties and shames, and carry on up the Khyber, living only in the present, waving not drowning. If I reproached myself for missing my chance, I told myself in self-justification that I could easily call on him to break the news when I visited Marshall.

So I never really had it out with him. I never taxed him with what he had done to my mother. I never said:

131

You hurt me. Parents, conventionally, are said to want the best for their children, but I think he was embarrassed by me, irritated, and probably bored. He wanted a buddy with whom he could have adventures, an ally with whom he could share his escapades, not a critic-in-residence. I think he saw me as a spy, smuggled in by the enemy under a diplomatic passport, reporting his secrets back to base.

He would die soon, and whatever it was that was not said between us would go to the grave, or into the air, or spinning round, unappeased, in my head. These are my problems. I have no doubt that, according to his credo, he had no regrets. He did not look at me and say, I wish I had known him better. He always laughed at the American obsession with self-analysis and said that he did not want to look too deeply into his psyche. He saw himself, I believe, as a slightly faulty engine that, despite everything, had made the journey in reasonable time without any serious breakdown. One of his many mottoes was, If it ain't broke, don't fix it. Civilisation, he would say, was about suppressing the primitive. And there was nothing quite as civilised, he would add with a wink, as a perfectly mixed Martini.

We finished our drinks and he escorted me to the head of the stairs, as I imagine he had escorted countless guests in the past.

'Thanks for coming, Sam. Good to see you. Regards to Ruth. Pip, pip.'

He limped away to find Jane and I was left standing alone under a gloomy portrait of a pear-shaped George the Third before the years of his madness.

19

The last time I saw Craig Marshall I thought that, despite everything, we almost managed to cross the rickety bridge of friendship together. I see now that I was deceived. He was just sorry for me. At the time I believed I had been forgiven. I never did entirely work out his relationship with Ruth.

Marshall was in his office, calmly seated at his desk, when I visited with him after the inquest. I had McCartney's gift to hand over, but I also wanted to say goodbye. On the face of it, I was just going home. Secretly, I wanted to be shot of the whole sorry business.

At first, he seemed remote, as if detached from his own personal drama. The broken vessel of his career was shifting on the seabed and what happened on the surface had no force or meaning. Slowly, as we talked, he came to life, though I found he was much quieter. His former agitation had disappeared. He was bitter, but resigned. 'People say I should fight, but they have no idea. I have been publicly accused, by innuendo and insinuation, and I cannot answer back. In a way, a court case, if it comes, will be a relief. I shall have a chance to be heard.'

I let him speak in this vein for a while. Marshall's office was clean, well-lit and clinical. Exotic fish darted up and down in an illuminated tank by the window. In the parking lot beyond, there was a steady coming and going of ambulances and private cars. Business appeared to be good. The wall planner above Marshall's desk indicated the occupancy of beds in the half-dozen institutions run by the group, including a hospice for the dying. I wondered vaguely if I should book a room for my father.

In his official white coat, Marshall was a commanding

figure, with the organisation of many lives in his hands, but the longer he talked the more I realised that inside he was a defeated man. He had a bunch of keys in front of him and, occasionally, as we talked, he would absently play with them, as if to reassure himself of his continuing freedom.

He was pleased I had seen McCartney, and grateful. 'Bob's a good sort,' he said. 'We went through a lot together.'

'He thinks the world of you.'

He smiled. 'No man is a hero to his valet.'

'He asked me to give you this.'

I handed over the flute. Marshall took it, laughing with pride and embarrassment and surprise. I could see he was touched. He tried a few notes, then put the flute on the desk and contemplated it warmly. 'It's nice to be reminded of your real friends,' he said. 'At the end of the day, there are so few you can rely on.'

I ignored this. I said: 'I also came to tell you I'm planning to go home.'

I had expected to surprise him, but he merely nodded. 'Ruth told me,' he said.

I recovered myself quickly. 'Is she pleased?'

'What an odd thing to ask.'

'I suppose you could say we have quite an odd relationship.' I don't know why I admitted that. It just came out. There was something about the neutrality of the room that made our conversation seem somehow off the record. I suppose that's what I mean about feeling a bond of friendship.

'That would appear to be something of a family speciality,' Marshall replied, with a thin smile.

'Odd relationships? What do you mean?'

'I think you know what I mean.' He was playing with me and enjoying my panic. He would always know more about Ruth than I could guess, and it gave him a temporary power over me. 'I'm talking about your father, of course.'

I relaxed. There was, I thought, nothing I did not know here.

'I'd say he's treated you badly,' he said. He seemed disposed to a calm but decisive frankness. I had the sense of a man with nothing to lose. He had been brought to the edge of a precipice and was resolved to speak his mind on everything.

'I'd agree,' I said, 'but I'm resigned to it now.'

He smiled again. He was like an actor who has had a private reading of the next scene of the script. 'What a funny family you are,' he said.

'Aren't all families a bit funny?'

'I believe some are funnier than others.' There was sadness in his voice. 'My parents are dead. Margaret and I have no children. I've told you the rest . . .' He made a circle in the air. 'Within these four walls, of course, I've seen it all. I never cease to be amazed at the secrets of the family. Is that funny? I don't know.'

'Some have more secrets than others.'

He nodded, apparently pleased with my reply. 'Yours, for instance.'

'Who told you?' For a moment I regretted what I had so lightly admitted. 'Ruth?'

He seemed surprised. 'Does she know?'

'I thought she might.' Whenever Ruth's name came up, I noticed, we went mutually on guard.

'You haven't told her?'

'Well, of course she's met Jane, but . . .' I reached the bridge in my mind I found it hard, almost impossible, to cross.

'But . . . ?' Now that my defences were down and I was retreating, Marshall was probing forward.

'But that's not the whole story.'

'No.' The keys chinked under his hand. 'No, indeed.'

The thought occurred to me that he was in the dark himself and was fishing for clues. 'Do you know Jane?' I asked.

'We've met.'

I wondered if he was lying. 'Where?'

'Here, as a matter of fact.'

Now it was my turn to express surprise. 'Here?'

His voice was quiet, but still firm. 'Her daughter has not been at all well, Seymour.' He spoke with sympathy, but it was the easy sympathy of the powerful.

'You mean, she's in your care?' There was, of course, no reason why she should not be, but I knew I sounded alarmed. I could not control myself. I looked wildly at the wall planner behind the desk to see if I could pick out Susan's name, but the writing was blurred and meaningless to me.

'She's being well looked after by the staff,' he replied, choosing his words with care. 'It's my job as administrator to visit the various units in the group. So . . .'

'I see.' I pictured Marshall sitting by her bedside, or strolling next to her in the day-room, quietly putting question after question, a scavenger picking over a forgotten life, looking for useful nuggets of information. 'Where is she?'

I saw he was going to make the most of this moment. 'Would you like to visit her?'

'Is it far?'

'Twenty miles.' He picked up the keys. 'I'd be more than happy to take you.'

I took a deep breath. I, too, was about to go under the surface. 'Thank you, Craig,' I said, getting to my feet.

'Oddly enough,' he said, as we walked down the corridor to the car park, 'we were about to close this unit. Then a bequest came in, out of the blue. Otherwise who knows where your sister would have gone?'

136

20

As I've said before, Marshall was always getting things slightly wrong. Susan is, of course, only my half-sister. For the record, we look nothing like each other, though the few people who know us both say that when I smile they can detect a family connection. I suspect this is fanciful. Instinctively, we want to believe in the gene pool.

Susan is much younger than me. She was born in the year Kennedy beat Nixon in the race for the White House. Her mother, the capable Jane, is a former Wren, part of the Beaver's entourage in the days when he was a regular Admiral. There is a story that the wardroom put up a case of Bollinger for the first man to take her to bed, but that is only Navy gossip. Jane was getting on a bit, but she certainly wasn't on the shelf.

What is not in doubt is that nine months after the annual round of Christmas parties, she gave birth to Susan. By this time, she had discreetly retired from the service and was living quietly on her own in London. Jane Bell was a proud woman, and an independent one. She did not press my father to divorce his wife (who was already living in the United States), or even publicly to acknowledge his indiscretion. She settled for a monthly cheque and moved to Hampshire where, in due course, she took up nursing. Locally, I understand that Mrs Bell, as she was known, was generally believed to be a Navy widow.

No one, in fact, knew the full story of Jane and her daughter, no one apart from discreet Mr O'Reilly, my father's lawyer, who dispensed the monthly allowance and became, as time went on, something of an uncle to the child. How often must such a story have been repeated within that respectable maze of social convention, the English Home Counties.

My father, meanwhile, was in the process of becoming an unconventional civil servant, 'seconded', as the rubric had it, from the Senior Service to the Ministry of Defence. Perhaps the business with Second Officer Bell also had something to do with his decision to come ashore for good. Of course, he continued to have his affairs with Judy and Camilla etc. and to perform what my mother called 'his less and less convincing impersonation of Peter Pan'. Even when, after several years, my mother and he were divorced (she thought she was about to marry the unsuitable Congressman from Atlanta) he kept Jane and her daughter, now seven years old, a secret from the other women in his life. My father is a man who is determined, as the Brits say, to have his cake and eat it.

Perhaps – and I suspect this was his hope – he would have taken this secret to the grave, but when Susan was twelve something happened. She was growing into a willowy, dark-eyed adolescent and had shown an unexpected gift for the piano. She had begun to study musical composition with a private tutor in London and there was already talk of a concert career.

What is the trigger that changes the inner configuration of the mind? The medical profession came up with a variety of names for Susan's condition, but essentially there was only one diagnosis. For several months, she went mad. When she began to recover, there was talk of an 'hysterical psychosis', but fairly soon the specialists seemed to agree that this was a case of schizophrenia, a term as darkly vague and frightening as any in the lexicon of ill-health.

My father's response to his daughter's crisis was typical. He was embarrassed by what was happening in front of his eyes, and I'm told he found it hard to discuss. But, deep down, he was an honourable man. He knew it was his duty to help, no expense spared. He invited Jane to come and live in the house by the sea. She was always referred to as the housekeeper and no one suspected anything different. Susan, who was in and out of psychiatric units as her condition fluctuated, had her own room, a piano to practise on, and the constant attention of loving parents.

In recent weeks, she had suffered what optimistic Jane called 'a setback' and was under temporary supervision again.

The Special Care Unit was housed in a rambling, half-timbered Victorian mansion on the top of a hill overlooking a wooded valley, a neo-Elizabethan pile set in a dozen acres of wild garden. Beyond the rose garden and the sundial, there was a lawn with an empty stone pool, an orchard, and a disused tennis court. Most of the patients had the run of the place and I believe that by the standards of psychiatric care in England it was an enlightened set-up.

It was late morning when Marshall pulled up in front of the house and parked his car in the space reserved for the administrator. The nurses were preparing to serve lunch and the smell of institutional cooking filtered into the hallway as we walked in.

Marshall was warmly greeted by the receptionist. He seemed popular. There was no hint of a reference to his recent troubles, though my presence was probably an inhibition. He explained that we had come to visit Susan Bell. I was introduced.

'How is she today?' I asked.

'Not so bad. I think you'll find her in the day-room.'

As we went through the baize door we heard the distant sound of the piano. I found I was apprehensive. I had met Susan only on a handful of occasions.

My anxiety was also stimulated by the broken-down ugliness of our surroundings, the smell and shabbiness of the place. A young man with a squashed-up face and a Fair Isle jersey too small for his body walked past, trailing a broom. Marshall explained that where possible the patients were encouraged to look after their living quarters. He pushed through another door and we passed a woman in a dirty print dress crouched on a wrecked sofa trying to read a letter. She stared at us vacantly and when Marshall said 'Hello, Shirley', smiled inanely, a grin from a Brueghel, a vision of hell.

The day-room was a former conservatory. We stood in the doorway, listening. Susan was sitting with her back to us, playing a classical sonata, I didn't know what. I looked away, towards the brightness of the windows. Outside, pressed against the glass, two other patients were peering in. Finally, she stopped. When Marshall knocked, she turned with a start.

'Susan, I have a visitor for you.'

'Oh.' She seemed put out, but far away. She stood up and came towards me, white and vacant as a ghost. 'Hello.'

I saw that she was struggling to recognise me. 'D'you remember?' I said. 'I'm Sam.'

I was conscious that Marshall was watching us together and wished, with some irritation, that he was elsewhere.

'Hello, Sam.' She did not at first realise who I was, and I could see her slowly make the identification as we spoke together.

'I . . .' Just for a moment, I was lost for something to say. 'I'm sorry we interrupted your playing.'

'I had to stop.' She picked the music off the piano. 'It's nearly lunchtime.'

'What were you playing?'

'Beethoven.' She smiled. 'He understands me.' She put the score into her music case and closed it. 'How's Dad?'

'He's fine.'

'Would you like to see my room?'

I looked at Marshall. 'I'm not sure . . .'

'Mr Marshall said I could move the chest of drawers under the window and put the bed behind the door, so I did. Before, the bed was against the wall and the noises from next door kept me awake. It's much better now.'

140

'That's good.'

'The girl in the next room is nice, but she takes things from the fridge. I have to keep an eye on her. I don't know why she wants to steal my food. She can't cook for toffee.' She laughed. 'Why are you here, Sam?'

'I came to see you.'

'That's nice. Are you staying for lunch?'

'I don't think so, not today.'

'There isn't time,' Marshall interrupted.

'The food here is okay, but I prefer Mum's cooking.'

'I expect you'll be coming home soon.'

'I'm glad you said that, Sam.' A sudden flash of anger passed across her face. 'Frankly, I think I've spent enough time here, Mr Marshall.' Tears came into her eyes. 'You've no right to keep me. I can leave whenever I want to. Everyone says so. Frankly, I think your behaviour is disgusting.'

'Susan.' Marshall remained calm. 'You know the doctors have to decide what sort of medication you need. Then of course you can go home.'

'He's right.' The storm faded as quickly as it had come. 'I have to have special treatment.' She smiled at me, wiping the tears out of her eyes. 'The doctor says I'm very special.'

'You are,' I said. I put my arm around her. 'You're very special.'

'Thank you, Sam.' She was touchingly self-possessed. 'I get very depressed here with all these loonies. Will you come and see me when I get home?'

'I'll try. I have to go to America first.'

She seemed puzzled. 'I thought Mum said you didn't live in America anymore.'

'No, I do.' I looked at Marshall. 'I do now.'

'One day I'd like to go to America. I'd like to see the Statue of Liberty, and Carnegie Hall and the Met. Will you take me to America, Sam?'

Marshall broke in again. 'You'll have to discuss that with your mother when you get home.'

Susan looked at me confidentially. 'The trouble with my mum is that she's terribly over-protective. She won't trust me to do anything for myself. That's crazy, isn't it?'

Marshall began shepherding us towards the door. He seemed anxious to be on his way and, as his passenger, I could not delay.

'Don't go, Sam,' said Susan.

'I'm afraid we have to. I have to go back to America now.'

I kissed her. Her cheek was cold and her fingers held my arm with a childish grip.

'You will take me to America one day, won't you?'

There was the sound of footsteps in the passageway beyond the day-room, and voices. The connecting door swung open and two nurses hurried in. One was middle-aged, the other, almost a teenager, could have been her daughter. Both looked alarmed. When they saw me with Susan they stopped, then looked at Marshall.

'Craig.' The older nurse was speaking in that calm way the members of the medical profession adopt when they are breaking bad news. 'You've got to come at once. There are two gentlemen in the hall to see you.'

21

Once Marshall had been arrested, his story passed into the public domain, and perhaps his fate was sealed. There was little I could do for him now. It was too late. He was in the hands of lawyers, free on bail, preparing his defence. The trial was scheduled for July. Within a few months he would be shut away in prison for a crime I believe he did not commit. More than ever, I wanted to get away.

My world was falling apart all over.

The week before Ruth and I took off for Spain, the Old Man suffered the ultimate humiliation, that fiasco in the desert. Surely someone could have tested those helicopters in storm conditions? The idea that the Southerner is a moron runs deep in America. The President had been so determined to prove he was not straight out of Dogpatch, Georgia. And now here he was, the peanut farmer from Plains, eating crow on network television, admitting responsibility for the failure of a mission in words that, in earlier, happier times, I might have written. The hostages seemed further than ever from freedom, and for the Old Man the writing was on the wall.

It was in these unhappy circumstances that Ruth and I set off on holiday together.

We flew to Toulouse and picked up a car, crossed the Pyrenees through the Roncesvalles Pass in a blinding storm and came down into the hot wheatfields of northern Spain, puttering along bad roads, over medieval stone bridges, towards Santiago de Compostela. As the days passed, and the sultry, decaying magic of rural Spain took hold, we recovered our spirits and began to enjoy ourselves again.

It was after Burgos Cathedral that Ruth announced she was tired of Roman Catholic guilt and wanted a swim.

We headed towards the coast. I was only too anxious to accommodate her whims. I wanted to please.

I have to say that she was in a funny mood. Warm and affectionate at some moments, cold and remote at others. Sometimes she seemed to be railing at me for my indecisiveness about my future, at other times glad that I was free, as she put it, to play.

I sat on the sand and watched her bobbing about in the waves. The water was freezing, but she did not seem to mind.

I watched her through the telephoto lens of my camera, and as she ran out of the waves I snapped her like a paparazzo. She raced up to me, wet and shivering, grabbed the towel and began to dry her body. I put the camera down and began to rub her myself, as I might have rubbed Alice or Charlie when they were little. She pulled my face towards her and kissed me hard. Then she put her hand into my trousers. We began to make love.

The beach was bare and the wind was whipping the sand into a fine gritty spray. We were quite alone. I felt as though we were reaching into ourselves deeper than for many months and when we drew apart again her expression was so dear and ruffled with the excitement of the moment we had achieved together that I picked up the camera and snapped her once more, in close-up.

(Here, on the Cape, the photograph is still hidden on my bulletin board.)

'I love you,' I said.

That was when she began to cry. It was only the second time I had seen her in tears, and I have to go back to the beginning to recall that first occasion.

144

1977

1

How many stories start in Paris? A great city is like a good host, bringing strangers together and making them welcome. The metropolis of art and leisure is a rakish old friend who turns a blind eye to our indiscretions. Is that the allure Americans feel? 'How romantic,' we say, as if the mere suggestion of love was sufficient explanation. There is, of course, the pleasure of strolling down boulevards free from the threat of violence. And then there's the myth of the place, spread by the GIs billeted here at the end of two world wars. We liberated the French, and they still liberate us. Anyway, it was in Paris that I first met Ruth.

I was on top of the world. I was thirty-two, married with children, and having the time of my life. I had a job that people dream about, working for the most powerful man on earth, as the newspapers say. He was to make his first official trip to Europe that spring, and everyone was watching. It's hard, now, to credit the excitement the President aroused in those early months.

Such journeys were always preceded, as you would expect, by an advance guard. On this occasion, I was part of that team. 'Sam's half English,' they said. 'He'll know how to talk to the natives.' On paper my job was to help draft the communiqués that follow a presidential progress, as seagulls follow an ocean liner. Most statements by world leaders are settled weeks ahead.

We were staying at our embassy in Grosvenor Square, keeping ourselves apart from the spooks and the diplomatic footsloggers. We were like fraternity brothers, high on achievement and success, and high on each other's company. We were cool guys getting the job done without trying too hard or taking it too seriously. We believed we could get away with anything, and we did. The Old Man had spoken of the lust in his heart, and been pilloried for it, but at the end of the day he was a decent guy who went to church on Sundays, prayed before meetings, and loved his wife and kids. Boy, did we compensate for that! We were boozing and screwing and bullying our way across the world like it was going out of style. When people speak about the absolute corruption of absolute power, believe me, I know what they're talking about. We were stinking.

On the weekend in question, we were still in London at lunchtime, combing through the small print of the forthcoming summit and smarting from a row Ambassador Young had been having with the British government. He had rashly accused the Brits of being 'a little chicken' on racial issues, and just then the last thing anyone wanted to do was to spend any more time than they had to with the supercilious smoothies from the Foreign Office.

We were sitting around in our room at the embassy, Herb and Walt and Jim etc., watching Red Rum win the Grand National for the third time, when someone said: 'What about Paris?' We decided this was a great idea, especially if we could get into the Ritz or the Georges Cinq. White House staffers always loved to intercut jags of work with jags of R and R. Our secretaries were sent scrambling for tickets, limos and hotel rooms.

I remember the flight was delayed and, when we finally took off, bumpy. Some of us overindulged on hospitality in first class. We arrived at the hotel with champagne hangovers and the blinding conviction that we were going to 'do' Paris come hell or high water. We were a conquering army again, Hemingway and Patton all in one.

So off we went, half drunk as we were, to La Coupole. Among so much noise and brightness and table-hopping we were just a gang of young American diplomats with a collective hard-on. Somehow, girls became attached to our party. I guess they could smell the power and money, and perhaps the stupidity. Herb used to say that if you worked at the White House and couldn't get laid you had to be as ugly as a horned toad. It was nearly midnight before we moved on to a nightclub, God knows where, on the Left Bank. By now we had tired of champagne and were doing vodka and a little coke. It was reported, from the dance floor, that the girls were giving tongue sandwiches. Finally, those of us who had not got lucky struggled back to the hotel in the small hours, vowing like big game hunters to do better the coming night.

When I woke later that morning it was raining, leaden, ominous rain. I stayed in my room and ordered up coffee and croissants. I had a speech to draft on one of the President's pet subjects, ecology and the environment, and I was reading up for it, ploughing through the dossier put together by our research department. I was becoming quite the expert on acid rain and Herb, in jocular moments, would refer to me as Doc Green. Sometimes, we would spend hours together browsing for suitable quotations. Now I come to think of it, he used to tease me about my 'Limey preference' for Shakespeare.

As it happened, it was quotations that got me talking to Ruth.

I was having tea, alone, in the luxury of the Ritz. The rain had stopped but I was in no mood for sightseeing. My colleagues had dispersed, with vague plans to meet for dinner. On the neighbouring sofa, there was this attractive Australian woman apparently flirting with an older man, possibly her sugar daddy.

I concentrated on my *thé citron*, read my *International Herald Tribune*, and from time to time tuned in to their conversation. I quickly realised that what I took to be flirtation was actually a high-octane interview technique in which the woman, whom I now knew to be 'Ruth', shared the secrets of her private life in the hope of extracting a confidence in return. An old trick. She spoke, I remember, with tremendous candour about a recent boyfriend. 'I mean, Neville, his breath! It was like making love to a dunny.'

The older man, Neville somebody or somebody Neville, was enjoying the performance and no doubt puzzling, as I was, if this was the prelude to more intimate suggestions. He was a handsome hulk of a man, a politician or an ambassador. In his big blue suit, he reminded me of a Texan rancher. His skin was the colour of polished pine. He had generous, outdoor features, a smile like a picket fence and a shock of bushy white hair.

By now I was eavesdropping quite openly and I was beginning to suspect that this Ruth was hamming it up for my benefit. She was blazing away, hard and bright as a connoisseur's diamond, waxy brown legs vanishing provocatively into a tight black mini skirt. As I discovered later, she had the country girl's need to impress the city folks, and always appreciated audience approval. She was in full flight on the subject of electoral corruption, when she lost the guts of a show-off quotation. 'What's that phrase? In blood, stepped in, something something. You know?'

Big Neville, outdoor type that he was, couldn't help her, and the poor old boy seemed a trifle unmanned.

Seizing my chance, I leaned across and said: 'I am in blood stepped in so far that, should I wade no more, returning were as tedious as go o'er.'

Old lockjaw smiled gratefully at me, and so did the girl, but in a way that said: 'Thanks, buddy, but keep out.' I guess she had some kind of scoop with this interview and did not want to be distracted. Her conversation was peppered with references to the CIA and someone called the Governor-General and I wished I knew more about Australian affairs. In those days hardly anyone in America knew where Australia was, much less cared about its politics.

Then, as chance would have it, old man Neville was

150

called away to the telephone and we were left alone together.

I asked her which Australian newspaper she worked for.

'I'm freelance.' She looked at me curiously. 'How do you know I'm Australian? Most Americans think I'm English.'

'Well,' I answered with a smile, 'how do you know I'm American?' I explained that my father was British.

'A closet Pom.' She considered me again, a representative of a suspicious species. 'You don't look like a bath-dodger.'

'You should see my dad.'

She found this amusing for no reason I could see. (Later, she told me: 'I clocked you for a boy with a bit of a father problem.') Her body was turned towards mine and she had put her notebook down. I'd not been dating for a while, being married and so forth, but I knew that if a girl laughed like that it was better than even money you could ask her out and not get turned down.

So I asked her out.

'You're quick off the mark.'

I could see she was impressed, and made some crack about being a young man in a hurry.

'Why not?' she said, almost to herself. 'Ruth,' she said, holding out her hand. 'Ruth Ritchie.'

'Sam Gilchrist.'

'Play it again, Sam.'

'Play it, Sam,' I corrected. She looked surprised, so I added: 'Quotations are my business.'

'What is your business?'

'I'm a speechwriter.'

'What's a speechwriter doing in the Ritz?'

'My boss sent me here.'

'And who's your boss when he's at home?'

I guessed she was imagining some old corporate fart. This was the moment I had hoped for. 'The President of the United States.'

'Fair dinkum,' she said, facetious and self-mocking. 'Fair bloody dinkum.'

151

I'm afraid I just smiled. As I've said before, working on the White House staff was always the ultimate seduction.

At this point Neville whatshisface came trundling back to continue the interview and I stuck my head into my newspaper. All I had to do was wait, and hope that the old boy didn't invite her up to look at his stamp collection.

Finally, she put away her notes, expressed shit-eating thanks for the opportunity blah blah blah, and escorted the old guy to the door. As she moved away, she gave a delicious wink and motioned me to stay put.

A few moments later I had the pleasure of watching her come towards me across the foyer, alone. As she sat down, she rolled her eyes, a gesture I came to know as typical.

'Where would you like to go?'

She looked me dead in the eye. 'This was your idea, Mister Gilchrist.'

2

As we left the hotel, I had the satisfaction of passing one of my hunting partners, Walt, coming in laden with expensive shopping bags from the Rue de Rivoli.

'Hi, Sam.' His greeting was a question I acknowledged but did not answer.

The taxi pulled away. Ruth looked back. 'Who was that?'

'Walter Coffin the Third. Descended from a Pilgrim family and about as white-shoe as they come.'

'Why do those kind of Americans always look as if they've been boiled in the bag?'

The taxi took a corner too fast, throwing us together. Ruth put her hand out and caught my arm.

'Isn't there an Australian upper-class equivalent?'

'Not that we admit to.' Laughter blazed out of her. 'I wouldn't really know any more. It's been ten years.'

I looked at her. She would be twenty-something. What was her story, I wondered?

She saw the look. 'I was born in Broken Hill, an outback town. I left Oz when I was seventeen. I ran away from school, lied about my age and went to Bali. Bummed around, slept around, washed dishes, hitched rides, took chances and ended up living in Bangkok. Then I got married, learnt how to write for the newspapers, got divorced, and drifted across to Europe. I bludged a job as a secretary, and then as a journo. Which is what I do now. You are in the presence of an upwardly mobile Australian.' She patted my arm. 'So there.'

The car juddered up the hill to the Sacré Coeur. As we got out, a belligerent young man with a monkey and a Polaroid camera began pestering Ruth. 'Oh, bugger off.'

She brushed him aside. 'And take your baby with you.'

A watery evening sun played across the slate roofs jumbled in front of us. The shape of Notre Dame loomed in the middle distance. To the right, a shower of rain was falling on the Eiffel Tower. Behind, the bells were chiming for vespers, or so I like to imagine. Ruth shivered.

'What stops you going home?' I asked.

'Too much to prove.'

It's true that I have rarely met a woman as competitive as Ruth. (Lizzie's upbringing would let no one hear the grinding of her personal axe.) For Ruth, everything was a challenge. She had to win. She had been born in the backwoods, away from the action, she felt, but Nature had compensated for this with the gift of an iron determination, a killer instinct that I, for one, found impossibly sexy.

We climbed the steps and strolled into the church. 'Doesn't it melt you to the coeur?' she said. Ruth adored puns, the more outrageous the better. Her articles were known for them, and in conversation she loved to play with the language. When I told her that we had a fellow called Doolittle whose sole task was to compose presidential gags, she was delighted. 'Doolittle, the court jester.'

I smiled. She had a way of putting things.

A service was in progress up by the altar. I said something smart-ass about the sentimentality of religion. 'I hate the Church,' she whispered. 'My parents are Catholic. They sent me to a convent school. The nuns were like the Viet Cong. That's probably why I lost my virginity at thirteen. To infuriate my father and scare the life out of my mother. By the time I was sixteen I'd had most of the boys in the neighbourhood.'

'It would seem,' I said, 'that you're fairly quick off the mark yourself.'

'It's not an experience I'd recommend. The Australian male's idea of sexual intercourse is to come as quickly as possible so they can go tell the blokes in the pub. Frankly, out in the bush, they don't care who or what's on the end of their dick.'

She always seemed disarmingly open about herself, but it was an invitation to share some candour in return. Sometimes, when I hesitated, she would say: 'Come on, Sam. Don't be a dag. You can trust me.'

I don't know why, but I did.

We found a bar and decided it was warm enough to sit, as Ruth put it, 'al fresco'. I liked the way she talked and, as a speechwriter, I was intrigued by the interrogative lilt she gave to the end of each sentence.

I ordered two beers. I must have been fiddling with my wedding ring because when the waiter withdrew she said: 'Tell me about your wife?'

'Lizzie?' I saw her in my mind's eye, tall, imposing, and serious-minded. Elizabeth Victoria Walker White. She is the daughter of a judge, a natural authoritarian who still scares the devil out of me. Five minutes in his company is sheer weight-loss. Lizzie is no pushover either. We met at the University of Pennsylvania, getting our MBAs, my one proper bid for respectability. She was by far the most sophisticated item on my personal agenda and, oddly enough, I, with my English connections and my year at Oxford, seemed exotic to her, too. Scratch an East Coaster and you generally find a closet Anglophiliac.

I said as much to Ruth, and then: 'I could hardly believe it when we started dating.'

'And the next thing you know, you're married.' She laughed that blazing laugh again. 'College sweethearts. Did you marry in church?'

'Bridesmaids, wedding march, champagne, confetti, and a drunk mother-in-law . . .'

'You make it sound so romantic.' She made a face. 'A far cry from my nuptial bliss.'

She had been married at nineteen to an English language teacher in Bangkok. 'A loud, stupid, drunken, fornicating

155

boor. The funny thing was, I loved him. He gave me the education I'd never properly had and did a lot for my self-esteem. Before Don I couldn't concentrate on anything longer than a menu.'

'How long were you married?'

'Three years. By the time I quit, I –' She paused, holding something back. 'I'd finished all of Jane Austen.'

'You quit?'

'He did a bunk to the islands with a little Thai scrubber. I thought, sod this for a game of soldiers and went walkabout. By the time the idle bugger had seen the error of his ways and come to his senses it was too late. I had the divorce papers served on him the minute he stepped off the boat.'

Ruth Ritchie was tough and driven. She had fought her way out of the sticks and, like Bronco, was taking no shit from anyone, no sir. Do I make her sound as hard as nails? I do not mean to. Ruth has a big heart, the wide, round eyes of an ingénue, and a kind of irrepressible animal charm. She liked to touch and flirt, and she wanted to win, but she wanted everyone to be on her winning team.

Now she said it was her turn to order the drinks. I said she seemed like one of the boys.

She thought about this. 'My father wanted a son. He used to play footie with me in the yard. He still calls me "mate". What about your old man?'

'He was a bit of an absentee.'

'Do you love him?'

'Love?' I looked down at my glass. It was not a word I associated with my father. 'I'd have to say I've grown fond of him, but I cannot forgive what he did to my mother. She left him in the end, but he broke her heart.'

'Is she still alive?'

'You bet! Ruling Georgetown society with a will of iron.'

'And you are the apple of her eye, I'm sure.' This time the lilt came with a tiny, complicit smile.

156

'It never feels that way, but yes, she wants the best for me. She arranged my job with the Democrats. We've had politics running in the family for generations.'

'When you're away, do you miss your family?'

I think we both knew we were heading into danger. I had always tried to be faithful to my wife, but here I was, alone with this attractive woman, the evening stretching ahead, talking about my marriage. I wondered exactly what was on her mind.

'I miss my children,' I said.

She asked for their names. Then she said: 'I had a child, but I lost it.'

This, I now recognised, is what she had nearly said before. I noted, as I often do, the secrets of the family. 'I'm sorry,' I said, looking her in the eye. 'You must have been very young.'

'I was pregnant when I married. In my head I told myself I wanted it, but my body gave another answer. I was so relieved.' She was suddenly shy. 'You think I'm horrible, don't you?'

I don't know why, but instead of answering I leant forward and kissed her. Our hands touched.

It was just a moment, a moment that the photographer with the Polaroid would have missed, but it was erotic and slightly scary.

'You shouldn't have done that,' she said, composing herself.

'I couldn't help it.'

'Don't say this is not how you usually behave.' The fierceness in her voice alarmed me a little.

'It's not,' I said, almost to myself. I looked at my watch. It was seven-thirty and darkness was closing in. 'Shall we go and find somewhere to have dinner? If you're not otherwise engaged.'

I knew I had to take charge. I sensed that for all her independence, she wanted the claim to be made. She wanted the men in her life to be men. Sure, I was up to the taxi, the drinks, and the dinner. The trouble would come later, when perhaps the limits to my courage would be exposed. Of course, at that moment, this was all in the future and neither of us could see clearly down the road we were taking. If we had, we might, with hindsight, have said No.

3

In two days, Ruth took over my life. Like any speechwriter, I'm exaggerating, but not much. Whatever the public relations people have to say, the stockholders of Seymour J. Gilchrist Inc. were more than happy to see new blood coming into the organisation from the outside. Who knew what unexpected dividend might not accumulate?

On Sunday night, when she joined our gang for a farewell dinner at a cheerful bistro down by the Quai d'Orsay, Ruth manoeuvred herself effortlessly centre-stage. She was quickly on flirtatious, first-name terms with Herb and Walt and Jim and Garry. Somehow she managed not to alienate the other women at the table, perhaps because part of her schtick was a merciless and frankly hilarious assault on the chauvinism and self-importance of my colleagues. Somehow, she got away with that, too. She told outrageous jokes, cracked execrable puns and got everyone to be candid about themselves in a way I had to admire.

I have to confess that, setting aside my admiration, this performance left me both jealous and apprehensive. We had only had one evening together and already I was just part of her audience. Sure, I was the object of much public stroking and touching, but I did not feel secure. Three of the men at the table were single and, worse for me, impressed. 'She's great, Sam,' said Herb, as we stood together in the men's room. 'What are you going to do when you get home?'

I did not thank Herb for articulating my dilemma. He and I were the married ones for whom such questions had the sting of reality. The others had girlfriends, but nothing so serious as to prevent a little fooling around on the road. Why not? A bit of extra fucking never did anyone any harm.

159

I have no doubt their women got their revenge in their own way. Washington is like that. There never was a town with so much sex in the air. A healthy young man with a good digestion and rudimentary social skills could wear out plenty of belt leather inside the Beltway.

'I don't know,' I replied. 'Pretend it didn't happen.'

'You've got the summit to look forward to.' Herb had quickly grown ambivalent about being in government. He had joined in the expectation of moving mountains, but had found that there was no real enthusiasm for change, just a lot of shit-shovelling and paper-pushing. In his cynical moments, he liked to say that if it wasn't for the school tuition fees, he'd be off in Maine running a lobster farm. There were a lot of guys like Herb in the White House, frustrated idealists with too much busy-work taking refuge in cheap cracks about the Georgian mafia.

'It's probably just a flash in the pan,' I said. 'Nothing serious.'

Herb was only tempting me with my own desires. The summit was barely a month away. Lizzie had made noises about bringing the kids and sharing the trip, but that was out of the question now. I would have to see Ruth. Just then, my one ambition was to get her alone for myself, and 'see' her every which way I could think of.

We went back to the table. Ruth was drawing a map of Australia on a napkin. I found myself standing behind her, with my hands on her shoulders.

'Gee,' said someone, 'it's awful big.'

'Any sharks in the ocean?'

'Here, but not here.'

'Why not?' I asked, asserting myself in the conversation.

'The crocs got them years ago.' She stood up, laughing. 'While you boys were shaking hands with the wife's best friend, we've decided we want to go dancing.'

'Why not?' I said, trying to conceal my disappointment. If I wanted her to myself, I would have to be patient.

We paid the bill and ordered taxis. We were Americans abroad. We assumed everyone spoke our language, English and dollars. Herb or Jim, I forget which, had this card, 'Le Chat Noir'. Our driver studied the address and nodded. As we set off, Ruth leaned across and kissed my ear. 'I want to go to bed,' she whispered.

The club was exactly as I feared, louche, noisy and overcrowded. A few couples were dancing to the slow, vamping music of a four-piece band, but most of the action was along the bar and in the dark, plush alcoves at the back and to the side. Our gang was quickly swallowed up in the scene. Ruth and I were left alone on the banquette. I took her hand.

'Where will you be tomorrow night?'

'London, I suppose.' She kissed me again. '*Et toi chéri?*'

I made a face. 'DC.'

'You'll be back.'

'I shall miss you.'

'Silly boy.'

She never liked sentimental talk. It implied too much. 'Let's dance,' she said, pulling me to my feet. We threaded our way through the tables to the floor. Herb, who was dancing with a brassy blonde, gave me a wink. I held Ruth close, possessively. We said nothing. The number ended and the band struck up 'It's All In the Game'. She knew the words and murmured them in my ear. 'Many a tear has to fall, but it's all in the game . . .' When it was over, she said: 'I want to get out of here.'

We said goodbye to the gang. I was glad to be getting away, if only briefly. Tomorrow, we would meet up again at Charles de Gaulle.

'You know something,' she said, as we strolled down the boulevard. 'I don't usually go out with people my own age.'

I had wanted to explore this before. 'How old was your husband?'

161

'My ex-husband,' she emphasised. 'He was thirty-five when we got married.' She broke her walk with a tiny, restless skip. 'I've usually gone for father figures of one kind or another. They're easier, you know, more attentive and more grateful, but you always feel you're missing something.' She put her arms round me. 'You're a nice change.'

'But I'm married.' I felt the panic rising inside me. 'I've got a wife and kids waiting for me.'

'I prefer married men.'

'Safer, right?'

She avoided my question, darting across the road towards a taxi. I noticed, as she ran, how quick and lithe she was in her movements.

When I looked at her again, in my hotel room, she was naked. 'I have to take a shower,' she said, stepping out of her clothes. She had a dancer's body, thin and tense, with soft, almost translucent skin. She was quite at ease with her own nakedness in front of me. I watched her walk into the bathroom and heard her gasp out loud as she stepped under the water. I took off my own clothes more slowly, and then followed her into the shower.

I slipped the soap out of her fingers and began to caress her all over, tracing her neck and her breasts and her thigh with my hand. The water and the soap ran together, foaming at our feet, and then, turning in my arms, she let me come into her, opening herself to me with a long kiss.

4

Twenty-four hours later I was standing among children's bath toys in the shower at home, cleansing my body of travel and, I suppose, of Ruth.

I was not alone. My son was at the age when he liked to watch me bathing. Through the torrent, I could see him sitting on the floor in his Snoopy T-shirt, my duty-free gift. As I stepped out of the water, he handed me a towel with page-boy courtesy. I yawned a thank-you and went into the bedroom for some casual clothes. Charlie followed, with questions about my trip. Just then, my children, whom I had said I missed, seemed to be an annoying intrusion.

'Can we go to England with you next time, Dad?'

I wondered if he had been put up to this by his mother. 'Not next time, but soon.'

'Do the English have big penises?' Charlie's current obsession was the size of the male member.

'Enormous,' I replied. 'They're well known for it.' I picked him up and carried him downstairs on my shoulders.

Lizzie was giving Alice spaghetti in the kitchen. She hardly looked up. 'Feel better?'

'Thanks.' I went to the refrigerator and cracked open a beer. 'Home sweet home.' I kissed my daughter. 'So – how were the kids?' Out of the corner of my eye, I caught Charlie mimicking my question to his sister.

'They've been very well behaved,' she said.

Charlie, always on the look-out for an advantage, took the opportunity to negotiate for a later bedtime. Alice joined in. Lizzie shook her head and surrendered. As I watched them race upstairs together I wondered what life would be like without them.

'Now,' said Lizzie, clearing away Alice's plate, 'I want to know everything.'

I looked at my wife in her apron, her hair pulled back, her eyes ringed with lines of maternal tiredness, and her cheeks flushed with the heat of the kitchen. There were thousands like her across the country, intelligent women coping with children and wishing it were otherwise. I felt sorry for her, and guilty in myself. I also sensed that intuitively she knew something had happened.

It's my job to put words into other people's mouths, but the invitation to speak for myself was unwelcome. I did my best, describing the diplomatic routine and the intricacies of our liaison work with the bland, big-bottomed representatives of Her Majesty's Government. As I spoke I realised that somehow I had to slip Paris into the conversation. If I omitted that, there would be trouble later, via the grapevine. Washington wives operate the fastest bush telegraph in the world. I'd agreed with Walt and the others that we could not possibly deny our excursion. 'So then,' I concluded, 'after we'd finished at the weekend, we flipped across to Paris.'

'Paris?' She checked, an edge of envy in her voice. 'Some people have all the luck.'

'It was okay, but nothing special. It rained. I mostly stayed in my room. The others went clubbing. Then we flew back.' I kissed her. 'And here I am.'

I made it sound simple, too simple, probably. At the time, I was impressed with my performance. I should have realised that she would not be taken in for long. Women have this sixth sense for errant husbands.

Sure enough, a little later we had the first awkward conversation on the subject of the approaching summit. This was the moment I had been dreading. We were sitting down to supper, alone at last. The children were upstairs asleep, bedtime stories told, rabbits and bears tucked in, Alice's night-light switched on.

Lizzie said: 'Why don't we come with you in May?

164

It would be fun for the kids and a nice surprise for your father.'

In hindsight, I should have welcomed the suggestion. I could have planted them safely in the West Country and made the most of Ruth in London. At the time, with her kisses still fresh in my memory, I prevaricated.

Lizzie's irritation was never far away. 'Don't you want us to come?'

'Don't be like that. It's just –'

'Just what?'

'You know what the President is like about . . .' I was about to say 'freeloading', but I stopped myself in time and ended lamely, '. . . this sort of thing.'

No amount of diplomacy was going to soothe her annoyance. 'For Christ's sake, Sam, I'm your wife. This particular President has driven us all nuts with his sanctimonious talk about the virtues of family life. He should be delighted that at least one member of his team is actually sleeping with his lawful, wedded wife.' She glared at me. 'Or have I got something wrong?'

I did not know how to reply to this, but I had jetlag on my side. I shook my head wearily and said perhaps we could discuss the question in the morning.

Each night that followed I would lie, in various states of wakefulness, remembering Ruth's passion. I guessed that Lizzie suspected something was not right between us, but she had nothing to go on. Ruth played the other woman's part to perfection: she did not write and she did not ring. That was my responsibility.

I had to choose a moment when I could catch her at home and yet not be interrupted by colleagues. I became familiar with the message on her answering machine. Occasionally, I would just say: 'It's Sam, ringing to say Hi.' On other days, we would talk. She would say: 'I can't wait for the summit.' Never did the diplomatic charade seem so vital. Herb and the other members of the gang would ask about her from time to time, but they never breathed a word outside. They were my buddies, and I could rely on them.

The days ticked by. Easter came and went. The blossom on the cherry trees by the Jefferson Memorial went candyfloss. Lizzie stopped pestering. The White House was running an austerity campaign. There was hot competition for seats on Air Force One. I was lucky to be going at all. Spouses were certainly not invited. The Old Man had just caused a big flutter among the media by selling off the presidential yacht, *Sequoia*. It was easy to play on Lizzie's ambitions for my career. If she came, we would have to find the money for it. I rang my father and surreptitiously enlisted his support. He agreed to invite us all for the summer vacation in August.

I realise now that I was in the grip of a sexual obsession. I had to see Ruth and have her/be had by her. Even now, when I think of her, I cannot stop my imagination running over the secret pleasures of our lovemaking. It was a wild, lustful quest for satisfaction, and I was a slave to it. I was discovering that the magnetism of sex is a destructive force that can leave a trail of devastation, broken homes and wrecked careers. But even as I write this now, I can appreciate the irony of these words: when I started with Ruth I never for a minute imagined. . . .

I took refuge in my work. For White House staffers, it was considered normal to be at your desk by seven-thirty, but there were some early birds who arrived at the Executive Office Building soon after six. I joined their number. I was rarely home before eight, often later. Sometimes it felt as though I went to sleep in that laminated plastic pass we all had to wear.

As it happened, there was no need for excuses. I was genuinely busy. Gone were the days when I simply churned out what we called 'Rose Garden garbage' – triumphant, high-flown speechettes for presidential delivery to Bible groups, women's clubs and veterans' associations. The President was preparing his 'moral equivalent of war' speech about the energy crisis. This was given on April 18th, barely three weeks before we were due back in London. Several of us worked on that speech, including the Old Man himself.

This performance was typical of my boss, stuffed with facts and figures. Designed to be morally uplifting, it had a tone that people found negative and puritanical. He talked of principles, but he did not touch people's hearts or even their imaginations. I had a sentence that said our future would be shaped not in Washington 'but in every town and every factory, in every home and on every highway and every farm', but that was as folksy as I was allowed to get. It was, I suppose, a brave speech, but it was the end of the honeymoon as far as the American people were concerned. There's a freebooting, Virginian side to our national character, and politicians temper that fire at their peril. The next guy in the job would have a far better understanding of how to speak to the nation.

A few days later, I rang Ruth as usual, in mid afternoon, Washington time. A man's voice answered. In my surprise, I almost put the receiver down, but recovered myself to ask for Miss Ritchie.

'Hold on,' said the voice, coolly.

Ruth came on the line. 'Hi there, pardner.'

'Hi,' I said, lowering the temperature some more. 'It's Sam. Is this a good time to call?'

'Of course it is.'

'What's going on?'

'Don't be stupid. A friend dropped by. I can't wait to see you.'

We chatted for a few minutes, and then I rang off. Now, of course, I know that it was Marshall. (Ruth has explained everything.) At the time, however, I was stunned. I imagined the worst. I realised I knew so little about her. Later that afternoon, after chewing things over in my mind, I rang back.

'It's me again. I'm sorry. I thought –'

'Don't think. Trust me. How many days is it?'

'Seven. I can't wait.'

'The Waldorf.' She laughed. 'Just the place for a romance.'

We talked on for some minutes, and then said goodbye. I sat at my desk wondering if she was alone now, or not.

5

When Air Force One touched down at Heathrow on the afternoon of May 5th, Stars and Stripes met Pomp and Circumstance. The Prime Minister was waiting at the foot of the steps to greet us, a kindly but shabby uncle who might treat you to a five-star meal and then hit you up for fifty quid. On the tarmac, with the jets screaming around us, the banal pre-scripted exchange of mutual esteem seemed more than usually absurd. Speaking from my notes, the Old Man referred briefly to 'the special and very precious relationship' between the two nations, conducted a handshake for the nightly news, and then followed the secret service detail to his bullet-proof Cadillac.

I swept into London behind the presidential cavalcade, the police outriders, limousines and blood wagon, a canoeist in the wake of a high-speed motor launch. The Democrats had not tasted power for years and we were enjoying that winning sensation.

There were flags everywhere. It was the Queen's Silver Jubilee.

You might imagine that I would be anxious about my contribution to the forthcoming negotiations. Even in an age of spy satellites and nuclear warheads, the right vocabulary can be surprisingly significant. So much can turn on the interpretation of a single phrase, so many deadlocks resolved by the substitution of a single word. Yet my chief worry as we came into the West End was not superpower diplomacy but condoms. I had left Washington in a hurry and in the dash to the airport had missed the opportunity to stop at a drugstore.

Perhaps Ruth would be waiting for me. Perhaps . . .

I wondered when exactly we would meet. We would not want to delay making love. That was the nature of our obsession. My plan was to check in at the hotel, then dive round the block and find what the English call a chemist's.

When I arrived at the Waldorf the concierge was looking out for me. 'I have a message for you, Mr Gilchrist.' I followed him to the desk. 'A young lady left this an hour ago.' I took the envelope, recognising Ruth's handwriting.

I decided to postpone the pleasure of her letter until I was alone in my room, but then I had a bad shock. Something unexpected had come up. She'd had to go to Northern Ireland and would be back in the morning. Northern Ireland! In the morning! I was only here for a few days. I'd studied my schedule on the plane and was already wondering how much free time I could snatch.

I was standing by the window, watching the toy traffic flow around the Aldwych. I crushed the paper angrily in my hand. I felt stupid and unwanted. What was happening in Belfast that was so important? I was so hyped up with the idea of imminent sex that just then I think I would have jumped the first person who walked through the door.

I looked at my watch. Six o'clock. I would kill time, calm down and go for a walk. I slipped out into the sunshine and drifted towards Covent Garden. The flower market had closed recently and the place was desolate, awaiting redevelopment. As I got into the rhythm of the walk, I began to feel more relaxed.

I have always liked the sensation of losing myself in the familiar bustle of London's streets. There is something about the city that allows visitors to shake off their identity and to enjoy themselves. There is none of the fear and aggression you get in New York. People potter, amble, loiter, and the sidewalk is a place on which they feel comfortable.

It was a warm evening and wherever I looked there were girls in summer dresses.

After the Piazza, I headed down Maiden Lane, towards St

170

Martin-in-the-Fields, crossed Trafalgar Square, that picture postcard, and struck out along the Mall, under the flags and plane trees, breathing in the coolness of St James's Park. The Royal Ensign was fluttering over Buckingham Palace, and official-looking black cars were sweeping in past the bearskin busbies in their sentry-boxes. On the corner there was a tour bus disgorging a party of senior citizens from the Sun Belt. I am not a snob, but I am sufficiently anglicised to admit that the experience of fellow Americans abroad can be more than slightly embarrassing.

I began the slow climb up Constitution Hill.

As I walked I thought hard about Ruth. Was this some sort of female test? But that, I reminded myself, was a false assumption. I was the married party. She was out in the world, a single woman. We had spent two nights together and spoken on the telephone perhaps a dozen times. We had not even declared ourselves to each other. I should relax and take things as they came. Why should I not be easy with her own super-abundant easiness?

I was strolling beside the Serpentine now, watching a mother and her two children paddling a dinghy in the grey-green water, throwing scraps of bread at the ducks. My thoughts went to Alice and Charlie. What would be their memories of childhood? What, for that matter, were they doing now? I looked at my watch. It was afternoon in Washington. They were probably playing in the yard, playing and fighting. Charlie was such a little boy.

I thought of my own father. Should I call him? That was always my dilemma. My feelings were so ambivalent, filial duty at war with filial rage. He would suggest a quick trip to the West Country. I would demur, with weasel excuses, and then we would fight. I resolved only to call if I had time to go visit. It was better that way.

On the bridge by the Serpentine Gallery there was a Mr Whippy van selling Mivvies and 99s, but I pressed on. Now I could glimpse the Albert Memorial through the trees,

171

and then the cookie-tin frieze of the Albert Hall. I remember my mother taking me there as a child to hear Britten's *Young Person's Guide to the Orchestra*. I'd been sick to my stomach, I don't remember why. Now I cannot look at that dome without an association of nausea and embarrassment.

As I crossed into Kensington the evening sun was slanting down the High Street in an aluminium glare, blinding the vision of homeward drivers in the rush hour west. I've never liked this neighbourhood, but London is a series of villages and you can always steer elsewhere. I turned south, through that maze of redbrick back streets, and ended up in Sloane Square. Sam Shepard's *Curse of the Starving Class* was playing at the Royal Court. I paused here, bought a couple of English newspapers and sat down on a bench to browse.

I was intrigued to find the press full of Nixon's TV interview with David Frost. How we are haunted by Watergate! Frost had pressed him hard and those famous jowls had shaken their historic denial. 'I don't go with the idea that what brought me down was a coup, a conspiracy. I brought myself down. I let down my friends, I let down my country, I let down our system of government.'

In the end, we all bring ourselves down.

As I turned the pages I thought, How small England is. Everyone seems to know everyone, somehow. And yet, at that moment, no one could reach me. No one even knew where I was. If I wanted I could vanish, I could disappear. At home, across the United States, thousands of people do this every year. They run out on family, home and job, cross the state line, drive for two or three days, and start again, making a new life. People say America is done for, but despite everything, the New World has not forgotten how to be new. The more I reflected on my situation, the more I realised that in England, as the song has it, you could run but you couldn't hide.

A couple of panhandlers were closing in. I got up, threw my newspapers into the trash can and moved on down the

King's Road. This, for me, has always been one of the great streets of London, a parade, a statement, a call to arms, a hang-out, a thoroughfare, a way to the West.

By the Duke of York barracks, I passed half a dozen teenagers, dressed in extraordinary clothes, torn shirts with bizarre slogans, torn jeans, razor-blades and safety-pins in ears and noses, Day-Glo hair, and satanic make-up. I had read about these people in American magazines, but here they were, a circle from some contemporary Inferno.

I wasn't frightened exactly, but I was disturbed. They seemed so alien, and so alienated. I would ask Ruth about them. Perhaps she had written about this phenomenon. Australian readers liked to hear about 'the changing face of Britain'. It was part of their complicated love-hate relationship that they wanted to be told how the mother country was falling to pieces. Deep down, deny it as we may, we all want to see our parents die, and to find our freedom.

What was Ruth doing in Belfast? I heard that male voice on the telephone, but surely it wasn't her ex-husband's? Was it someone she had not mentioned? I knew I was being absurd. The jealous lover cuts a ridiculous figure.

I reached the bend in the road, and a slogan on the wall of a municipal building, TORIES WANT WAR. I decided to go no further. There was a public house, the Water Rat, invitingly open. I would have a drink. English ale, warm and bitter and strangely likeable. There were more weird-looking teenagers in black hanging around outside, and others with ripped clothing in the street opposite in front of a store called Seditionaries. At the next table, two old men were playing checkers, as they had presumably done for years. They had, I imagined, seen a dozen changes of fashion, Teds and Mods and Hippies, and now these Punks. On this view, the Jubilee was not a richly embroidered national pageant, but a brilliant weed sprouting between the cracks in the imperial façade.

I drank my beer and then went to the men's room. As I

173

relieved myself, I noticed a rusty machine selling condoms, fifty pence or five tens. But I didn't have the change and anyway, tonight, I didn't have the need.

6

I had briefed my colleagues in advance about the crisis in Britain, the bankruptcy and demoralisation of the state, but nothing I said could have prepared them for the dimness and lethargy we found among our opposite numbers on the British side. We were like a professional football team playing away in an amateur league. Some of us found it hard to suppress our amusement and disbelief.

We met early the next morning in the conference room of some godforsaken office building, the department of something, not far from the Palace of Westminster. As the meeting went grinding on, I noticed how our counterparts had this habit of blaming their cock-ups on other people. Psychologically speaking, they still managed to sustain an air of weary superiority.

During the session, we were served with weak institutional coffee and dry biscuits. Walter, who fancies himself as a bon vivant, rolled his eyes and said to the organiser, a military man with a chewed grey moustache, 'If this is tea, I'd rather have coffee.' Our hosts were not amused.

At eight-thirty, after an hour of pomposity and pettifogging, we went back to the hotel to prepare ourselves for the meat of the day's agenda.

I was on the point of leaving my room to rejoin the others in the foyer when Ruth telephoned, bubbling with apologies. She was still in Belfast, but hoped I could be free that evening. I suppressed my annoyance at her absence. 'It would have to be late,' I said, studying the schedule.

'Perfect.'

'What's going on?'

'I'll tell you when we meet. You won't be disappointed. Do you know the Hilton?'

I began to stumble. 'Why – ?'

'Trust me,' she said. 'I'll see you in the lobby at ten.' I caught that upward inflection in her voice, and the hint of laughter. 'Promise I'll be there. Bye.' Ruth was always speedy, impressionistic and demanding, but somehow she got away with it.

I did not have much time to brood on the enigma of Ruth's absence. While the worker-ants prepared for the summit in London, the President was scheduled to pay a visit to a village near Newcastle upon Tyne, the home, it was alleged, of George Washington's ancestors. We speech-writers had done our homework and given the Old Man a curtain-raising line, Ha'way the Lads, calculated to melt every Northern heart. For once this bucket of country corn worked wonders with the press as well. The Old Man basked in golden headlines. The honeymoon was still on, at least in Europe.

In the evening there was a dinner for heads of state at 10 Downing Street, but no speeches were planned and I wasn't on call. But I was hardly off duty. I had cribsheets to prepare for the first full day of the summit in the morning.

I was happy to be at my desk amid the chaos of the travelling White House. I had decided to test Ruth by arriving late for our rendezvous.

I have stayed in Hiltons the world over. They are like small pieces of America set down in alien territory, vital refuges from the barbarian ways of abroad. In the Hilton, we know the shower will always work, the coffee shop will sell *Time*, *Newsweek* and ice-cold Coke, there will be telephones and taxis we can rely on, and a menu you can understand at a glance. A Hilton is a home from home.

Ruth was pacing up and down the foyer in sandals and a short black dress. She had been swimming and her hair was damp. I guessed from the way she swung her legs as she walked and flirted with her movements, that she was naked under her dress. When she saw me she ran impulsively across the lobby to greet me. We kissed, and kissed again. I held her fiercely to me, feeling the warmth of her body. 'Come on,' she said, and took me by the hand into the bar.

We ordered two exotic cocktails and set ourselves apart from the other drinkers. We kissed once more. 'You look well,' Ruth said.

'All the better for seeing you.'

There must have been a note of reproach in my voice because she apologised for her absence again, adding that she had a rather extraordinary story to tell.

Some people attract stories, just as others can live incident-free lives of blameless equilibrium. Ruth was a woman who liked the idea of adventure and in some senses went looking for it, too. She once told me that she would do things on the spur of the moment, simply for the thrill of it, to see what would happen next. I called it 'driving on empty'.

'Listen to this,' she said, as the drinks arrived. 'Three years ago when I first came to London I was flat broke. I'd had the promise of a job in a publishing house that fell through. So I signed on as a temp typist. The first thing that came up was a job with an estate agent in the Fulham Road. As it happens, they were short-handed and I was called in for several weeks at a stretch. You may not know this, but it's common practice in that business to put women like me in the window to attract clients.'

'I wonder why,' I teased, and kissed her again.

'So I'm sitting there like a secretary bird when I'm aware there's this guy standing outside, pretending to look at property but staring at me through the glass. He's not bad-looking, but middle-aged and conventionally dressed in a suit and tie, and carrying an umbrella and briefcase. I

177

ignore him of course and he goes away. The blokes in the office have a good laugh about it and I think, what the fuck, I'm only temping. The next day I look up from my work and there he is right in front of me, asking about residential leases. I say, You'll have to talk to one of my colleagues. He says, They're busy. So I say, Then you'll have to wait. He seems disappointed, but he accepts this and in due course I pass him on to my boss. He has a Scots accent I rather like, and although I probably make him sound pushy he actually seemed a bit lost and out of his depth in a strange sort of way. The next day he's back again, and I'm not even surprised. It's the lunch hour. I'm alone, holding the fort by the switchboard. I ask him how he's getting on. Fine, he says. He seems distracted. Suddenly he says, Will you have a drink with me after work? I think, This is dumb. He must have seen something in my face because he says, You can rely on me, I'm an Army officer.' Ruth laughed. 'What a recommendation! Then he introduced himself as Major Marshall from such and such a regiment and explained he was at a loose end in London. He certainly seemed lonely enough. Well, I think, he seems a decent sort of bloke. I say to myself, Life's short, and then you die. Why not?'

'Who is he?'

'I'll come to that. To cut a long story short, we arranged to meet at the Lamb and Flag the next day. I was delayed, and when I arrived he was already at the bar, dressed up to the nines in one of those old-fashioned suits with wide lapels. There's something out of date about him, as though he's not fitting in anywhere. We have a couple of drinks and I ask him why he had picked me up. I mean, why me?'

'You remind me of my first wife,' he said. 'It's as simple as that.'

It turned out, as he unfolded his story, that as a young man Marshall had been married to a Glasgow girl, Molly. He was a junior officer. They'd been posted to Malaya and she had been killed in a freak road accident involving an army jeep. He had been devastated by her death and thrown himself into service life. Finally, in the late Sixties he had been posted to Ulster, where he had married for the second time. Now, he was over in London 'on business', but wondering if he could afford to switch careers. He had been scouting for property when he saw Ruth in the estate agent's window. He couldn't believe how much like his late wife she was, and had decided that this was a sign.

They had another drink and he asked Ruth about her brilliant career, as she put it, but he seemed somewhere else. Suddenly he said: 'Do you fancy a spot of gambling?'

He was, he said, a member of this casino.

'I'm thinking, This could be dodgy, but he seems okay, and, what the hell, I agree.'

So off they went, gambling.

Ruth told me Marshall took her to this joint in Soho, a place called Charlie Chester's. He had lost money, not much, and Ruth had beginner's luck, winning enough to suggest they have a meal to celebrate. 'That's all it was,' she said. 'A fun night out for two lonely people with time on their hands. I didn't discover much more about Marshall, except that he was based in Northern Ireland and didn't like the way things were going there. He kept on saying that he was sure his luck was running out, but I didn't know what he meant, exactly, and to be frank I wasn't that bothered.'

'Did you see him again?' I asked.

'That's the interesting part. He said I should call if I was ever in Belfast. I put his number into my contact book and forgot all about it. Then six months later, I'm working for newspapers now, I get this call. He's in London again. His boss has given him two tickets to the opera. Was I free?'

'Some kind of boss.'

'That's what I thought. I found out that Marshall was moving on the edge of a strange circle of upper-class Army types.

He seemed to think it was normal enough. One minute he could be interrogating terrorists in top-security barracks and the next listening to Joan Sutherland. I remember thinking, as we sat in these incredibly posh seats in Covent Garden, that military men are not at all the way you'd reckon.'

Ruth paused, as if hesitant about something.

'What's the problem?'

'I fucked him,' she said. 'I couldn't stop myself – it was just a mad moment. There was something so dear and unreachable about him, something so vulnerable and so lost. I wanted to see – oh, I don't know, why do I have to apologise, I fancied him, why not?' She shrugged. 'I told you I like older men.'

'And now?' I sounded calmer than I felt.

'It was only one night. We both knew there was nothing in it. He loves his wife. He soon realised I was nothing like his Molly.'

I took her hands in mine and kissed her. 'I love you,' I said.

'And you, naughty boy,' she said, 'you're married.'

'So was he.'

She looked away. 'For some reason, that didn't seem to get in the way with him. I'm sure he's had more than one woman like that, hardly knowing he was unfaithful. He invites it, you'll see.'

'Perhaps he can give me lessons.'

'I don't think he understands his effect on people. In some ways he's easy to manipulate. He's really just an innocent, without a trace of calculation.'

'He sounds incredibly naïve.'

'I suppose he must do. That's part of his appeal.' She sighed. 'That was the night he began to tell me about his life.'

I was about to interrupt, but she stopped me. 'I'm not going to tell you myself. I'd get it wrong. But he will.'

'I don't understand.'

'He wants to meet you,' she said.

The Hilton rendezvous suddenly made sense. 'Is he coming here now?'

She shook her head. 'I'll explain. When you rang the other day, that was him. He'd turned up on my doorstep that morning. He was over for a meeting. He wanted my help, as a journo. He's in the middle of a dispute with his superiors. That's why I had to go to Belfast.'

'Why should he want to meet me?'

'While I was over there I explained about you. I wanted him to be clear about things.'

'Things?' I wanted her to admit something.

'Our relationship. When I told him you worked as a speechwriter for the President he got really excited. In some odd way, he seems to think you are the answer to his prayers. He's got it into his head that you can help him with his story.'

'But Ruth, this is crazy.' I could not disguise my exasperation. 'Just because I work in the White House, it doesn't mean . . .'

Ruth finished her drink. 'Do me a favour and see him.'

Perhaps if I agreed we could drop the subject, go back to my hotel and make love. 'When?'

'Tomorrow evening.'

I was relieved to be able to say at once that I couldn't do it. 'Tomorrow's the big day.'

Ruth was not dismayed. 'Well then, when?'

I searched my schedule in my head. It would have to be Monday at the earliest. The summit would be over by then. Under pressure I agreed that I could persuade Walter or Jim to cover for me. 'Where?'

'You'll have to be patient, Sam.' Her eyes betrayed further complications. 'He believes he's being followed, and says I may be under surveillance, too. That's why he insisted I meet you here.' She shrugged. 'What can I tell you? It's what he believes. He says we have to meet out in the open. He's

181

suggested a rendezvous at Charing Cross Pier. Six o'clock. His idea is we take the ferry to Greenwich. You and I will go on board as tourists. He'll be there already, waiting for us.'

'This is bizarre,' I said, but I agreed.

As we walked out through the foyer of the Hilton I wondered who was watching. Ruth's story seemed fairly extraordinary, but I'd seen enough political dirty tricks at home to know I should cool my scepticism.

Later, in the small hours, when Ruth was asleep, I left the bedroom and, closing the door behind me, slipped across my suite to the telephone by the TV screen. On the digital clock it was two-thirty.

'How's it going?' Lizzie was invariably practical.

'I've just gotten in.' I spoke quietly. 'I called to say I love you.'

'I love you too.'

'How are the kids?'

'Fine. They ask where you are, but we watched the news together and I think they understand you're with the President. When will you come back?'

'It's kind of open-ended. I guess I should call my father. He'll know I'm in town. I may go and see him while I'm here.'

We talked about family matters for a few minutes. I was beginning to feel the night's chill. Finally, I signed off. 'Love to the kids.'

'Big kiss, sweetheart.'

'Big, big kiss.' I waited for a moment. I heard the click at the other end and then I, too, quietly replaced the receiver.

'Big kiss.' Ruth was standing in the doorway, quite naked. 'All you men are the same,' she said. 'You want it both ways.'

I began to protest, but I was caught red-handed, without an alibi. 'You know what kids are like,' I said, and I

182

knew I sounded as lame as a busload of paraplegics.

'And husbands, too,' she replied. 'In the end, you have to choose.'

7

The Greenwich ferry was waiting in the shadow of the Embankment when Ruth and I, separating ourselves from the rush-hour crowds, hurried down the gangway of the Charing Cross Pier. 'Don't look now,' said Ruth, as we stepped on board, 'but he's on the upper deck.'

'I wouldn't dream of it.' I handed our tickets to a pimply boy, and led the way down to the lower level. We had agreed we would not make our rendezvous until we were well under way.

The boat was not crowded. Besides ourselves, there was a scattering of sightseers in anoraks and plastic macs, a school group, and one or two old people. Ruth was in sneakers and a heavy sweater. I felt conspicuous in my suit and tie, but there had been no time to change. I had broken away from the final press conference, explaining to Herb that if anyone asked for me I was dealing with a family crisis. 'A family crisis?' He looked at me with amusement. 'I suppose that's one way to describe adultery.' I was too preoccupied to put him straight.

Big Ben struck six. As the chimes faded, the ferry's propellers began churning the water. We manoeuvred onto the tideway in the shadow of the bridge, swung in the current, found our course and began plugging downstream.

The river was filling up and there was sun on the water. The panorama of the City was before us, churches and office blocks to the left, empty warehouses to the right. Water traffic buffeted through the choppy brown water. Ruth took out a pocket camera. A Japanese tourist offered to take a picture of us both against St Paul's. When Tower Bridge came into view, I suggested it was time to go find Marshall.

He was sitting up in the bow, a solitary figure, staring ahead like a lookout. Ruth came and sat herself opposite, and I joined her. 'This is Mr Gilchrist,' she said.

We looked at each other and shook hands. I'll never forget Marshall's expression, a mixture of deadpan gravity and boy scout vulnerability, or his handshake, which was a real bonecrusher.

'It's good of you to come,' he said, as if he meant it. His voice was mild and Scottish, as Ruth had said. 'How's the summit going?'

'No surprises. That's the main thing.'

'I hope,' he replied, 'we shall have no surprises here.' He looked round. 'Do you think we are alone, so to speak?'

I turned involuntarily. There was a chill wind off the Thames. The front deck was deserted. Above us, steering in the warm, the captain was chatting to the pilot. We agreed that even if we were overlooked we could not be overheard.

'You probably think that this behaviour is rather paranoid, Mr Gilchrist,' Marshall began, 'but when I've finished perhaps you'll see why it's best to take precautions.' He gestured at himself. 'I'm a military man, Mr Gilchrist, I was brought up to be on guard. I've been a soldier all my adult life, but recently I've been fighting battles I don't believe in.'

'Ruth tells me you're based in Northern Ireland.'

'And have been for many years. Don't get me wrong, Mr Gilchrist, I believe it's right to have the Army on station there. Besides, I like the place, odd though that might sound. I like the people. The work is real. It's better than shuffling paper across a desk in Whitehall. At least we have an enemy of sorts to fight. People forget that soldiers join up in the hope of action.'

Marshall's words were interrupted by a long blast from the ferry as we passed under Tower Bridge. Across the water, the famous fortress seemed small and toylike. A Union Jack flapped against the flagpole on the White Tower.

Marshall was looking at me as though he was unsure about

telling me his story, and perhaps in retrospect he was right to be sceptical. I must have seemed young, strange and slightly foreign. There was also the fact that Ruth was holding my hand.

'There's so much to explain,' he said. 'It's hard to know where to start.'

'Just tell me what happened to you, from the beginning.' I pointed upstream. 'We have plenty of time.'

The interminable waterway, the Thames, was opening out in front of us, winding wider and wider, between empty docklands and hazy mud-flats, a luminous invitation to go on and on, and further, towards the open sea itself.

'I grew up in a little village near Inverness,' Marshall began, 'and as far back as I can remember I wanted to go into the Army. As a boy, I would read about the heroism of the Highlanders in battle against the English, or the glorious deeds of Scottish regiments in the far-flung parts of the British Empire. That was the life I wanted. As soon as I could I enlisted. I was eighteen. It was the year of the Queen's coronation. We watched it in the mess. It was the first time I'd seen television.'

I guessed, as he spoke about the Army, that as well as its camaraderie it also provided an automatic society in which, so long as you played your part, no one would trouble you with difficult choices.

'People say Army life must be boring. Not to me. I was as happy as larry in the ranks. The Army was my travel agent, my university and, as it turned out, my matchmaker, too. Soon after I joined up I fell in love with Molly, the colonel's secretary. We were married within the year.'

I exchanged a glance with Ruth, and Marshall caught it.

'Yes, she was indeed like Ruth, slim and dark and full of laughter, a beautiful girl. As I'm sure Ruth has told you, she was taken from me in tragic circumstances shortly after I was posted to Malaya.'

I gave a sombre nod. I saw a green wall of tropical

vegetation. I saw a brilliant butterfly and the raucous buzzing of insects, the sticky warmth of the jungle, and a young man in uniform weeping by a simple grave.

'I thought I would go mad with grief. Now I needed the Army more than ever. I threw myself into my work and rose up the ranks. I had nothing else to live for, not even children. Molly was pregnant when she died, but the baby did not survive.'

He paused and looked away. The water rushed under the prow. Overhead, a silver jet was circling in descent, so small and clear against the sky it was as though you could reach up and touch it on the wing.

'By the late Sixties I had reached the dizzy height of major, but I knew I was not likely to go further. That was when our troops were sent into the North. My regiment was among the first. I suppose because I'm a Scottish Protestant I understood the situation better than some.'

He took out a silver cigarette case, in a way I came to associate with him, and lit up. Ruth and I refused.

'Frankly, I was fascinated by what was happening. It was a bad time, but I didn't find it grim. We were giving it all we had, and so were they. I think my superiors saw my enthusiasm. They fixed me up with a car, a house and a driver, and gave me carte blanche. Then I met my present wife, Margaret. You could say that nineteen seventy-two was the year I began to put my life together again.'

We were quiet for a moment. The voice on the Tannoy was pointing out historic features among the docks. Now, as I write, this low bight is being developed as a showcase for the new capitalism, but in those days it was empty and silent, haunted by the ghosts of a seagoing empire. To left and right the flat horizon was dotted with the spires of Wren churches and a few disused cranes. Gone was the hum and clatter of a great port at dusk.

Marshall was speaking again. 'I joined one of the Army's most secret units. The province is so small and the people so settled you can keep the entire population under surveillance. Then you carry out what we call psy-ops. The idea is to turn a psychological understanding of the situation to military advantage. My job was to be the public face of the team. I was to brief the press, handle visitors and arrange tours for politicians and generals.'

It occurred to me, as he spoke, that our lives were oddly parallel. We were both, in our different ways, on the edge of the big picture, watching history from the wings.

'I liked my job,' he went on. 'I discovered I had a gift for stories the press would believe. I was an only child. My early life was full of imaginary friends. I have always been at home with make-believe. My rule with journalists was to be accurate ninety per cent of the time. Then they would believe me. Besides, they could see I had the ear of the high-ups. Every now and again I would run a story that would hurt our enemies. A lie. It was a game and something of a challenge intellectually. I'm afraid I enjoyed seeing my inventions reported as hard news in the national press.'

A young man and his girlfriend strolled up and leaned on the rail in front of us. Marshall paused. It was my turn to speak. 'When you've finished your story,' I said quietly, 'you'll tell me what I can do for you.'

He nodded, but did not speak.

Ruth pointed. 'There's Greenwich.'

The masts of the *Cutty Sark* were visible ahead, then the Naval College, and then the Royal Observatory.

'I read somewhere,' said Marshall, 'that in the old days before a long voyage sea captains would set their chronometers by the clock in Greenwich.'

'And now this is where Time stands still,' said Ruth. She never could resist a crack against the Brits.

Other tourists joined us at the bow. We stood up, mingling with the crowd. The rest of Marshall's story would have to wait.

The ferry berthed alongside the pier with a creak of

timber. On the timetable, it was scheduled to return upriver in an hour. There was time for a drink and a stroll through the cobbled back streets. We watched the crew dexterously complete the mooring, then I took Ruth's arm and we came ashore. As we left the quay, Marshall took up my invitation.

'I want you to understand, Mr Gilchrist, that Northern Ireland is only the beginning of the story. It's merely the context for what happened next. What I have to tell you about is something that concerns people who live here in England. I'm conscious that I cannot write this story myself. You are used to putting words into the mouths of others. I'm hoping you might be interested to consider doing this on my behalf.'

I looked at Ruth.

She kissed me, reading my thoughts. 'Of course I could do it, but I don't have your position.' She glanced at Marshall, as if rehearsing a line they had already agreed. 'I think you'll find that when he's finished his story you may have a strong personal incentive to take up his invitation.'

8

There were fewer travellers on the return journey. Darkness was closing in and most of the passengers were crowded below, near a small, half-lighted bar. We stayed on deck in the cold. The ferry pulled out onto the Stygian waters and the lights of Greenwich grew small in our wake. Ahead, in the distance, was the orange glow of the city. A white moon was rising, as full as the tide. How many vessels had ridden this flood? How many tales had been told out here? Once we were under way, and far onto the river, Marshall continued his narrative.

'I became a master of the art of black propaganda. As time passed, there was no dirty trick to which we would not stoop. We would do things over there we would not dream of doing on the mainland. And yet, despite all our best efforts, we could only scotch the snake, not kill it. More and more people in the Army were beginning to say that the problem was not military but political.'

'When was this?'

'This was soon after I married Margaret. That's seventy-three and seventy-four. It was a time of crisis here. I expect you remember the miners' strike and the three-day week.'

'That was when I arrived in London,' said Ruth. 'You guys had two elections, and I hadn't registered in time to vote in either. Did I feel colonial, or what?'

'We had a few problems of our own that year,' I said. I was working for the Democrats then, and was pistol-hot with self-righteous talk about impeachment.

'That's true.' Marshall was not really interested in American politics. He was pursuing his own line of thought. I sensed that he was relieved to be able to speak of these matters. 'No one seemed to be in charge, and no one seemed to have the will to take a firm line, either in Northern Ireland or at home. After a few drinks in the mess, you would find officers saying that the real enemy was not the Irish but ourselves.'

'Did you believe that?' I put my arm around Ruth. The boat changed course slightly. A massive black lighter, loaded to the gunwales, with a single yellow light on the prow, thundered heedlessly upstream.

'Army officers have said things like that,' Marshall replied, 'since the beginning of time. Soldiers have always despised politicians. But here, for the first time in my career, I saw people begin to imagine that it was their duty to speak out and do something. You'd hear people say that it was time to stand up and be counted. They're very dangerous, the whispers of duty. And what was really dangerous, we had the skills and backup to do it. Out there in the province, when no one was paying attention, we'd created this machine we could use against ourselves.'

There comes in all good stories the state of mind we call the suspension of disbelief, that moment when the storyteller carries his or her audience from the world they know and recognise into the place where Gawain meets the Green Knight or where Cinderella is whisked away by her Fairy Godmother to meet Prince Charming. Marshall had boasted of his skill at persuading journalists to suspend their disbelief and publish information that, in their better moments, they must have doubted. I told myself I was different. Perhaps because deep down I was afraid of the direction his story was taking, I continued to resist the things he was telling me, things I now acknowledge to be true. And yet, despite, or perhaps because of, my scepticism, I did not stop him.

'There was at this time,' he went on, 'a popular television comedy series with the catch-phrase, "And now for something completely different." '

'Monty Python's Flying Circus.'

191

'You've seen it.'

'I expect Ruth has told you. I come over here from time to time. My father is English. We've watched it together.'

'Yes,' he said. 'I know about your father.'

I wanted to interrupt, but I decided to listen. It would be interesting to hear what he had to say, unprompted.

'We used to watch this programme, avidly, each week. That catch-phrase became part of our vocabulary. "And now for something completely different," we would say to each other. In a funny way, I think it helped us to make the leap, to think the unthinkable.'

'When you say "we", how many were involved?'

He hesitated, as if counting in his head. 'Perhaps a score in the province itself, and maybe a dozen here. I'm sure there were several more who were aware of what was happening and who simply turned a blind eye.' He looked at me. 'You say "were", Mr Gilchrist, but I must make it plain that it's not over yet. Some of these people are still active, as I know to my cost.'

I nodded. 'Tell me what went on,' I said.

'We began in a small way, almost by accident. At first, we were simply obstructive. If there was a peace-making initiative from the politicians, what we would regard as a sell-out, then we made sure that it didn't stand a chance. Our unit could discredit anything. There were so many lies and counter-lies in the air it was impossible to trace our efforts. And there were plenty of people in the province, of all colours, who were only too happy to help us.'

I looked at Ruth.

She was listening hard, and well understood the significance of what he was saying. I wondered how much she cared. Didn't she, as I did, secretly want to be back in my hotel room? (As I recall this scene now, I remember my frustration.) What was her interest in Marshall's story? Why could she not perform the assistance he was looking for? Why did it have to be me? As the evening unfolded I was beginning

192

to suspect there was an answer to this question, but I should make it clear that it was not until later that I got a definitive explanation.

Marshall was pressing on. 'The truly scandalous side of our activity occurred when we started to turn our efforts towards the mainland.'

'What sort of efforts?'

'We would disseminate lies about public figures we believed to be responsible for the failure of strong government. You might be surprised to know how easy it is to leak disinformation to the press, especially if you are speaking off the record on behalf of the security services.'

'What sort of lies?'

'That X has been talking to the Russians, that Y has a Swiss bank account, or that Z likes little boys. We planted these and many other such stories, and in their different ways each caused a great deal of damage to the leadership in both parties.'

I turned to Ruth. 'Have you read any of these stories?'

She saw the doubt in my face. 'Yes,' she said, becoming serious. 'I've also seen documents that support the case.' I felt a pressure on my arm. 'You can't ignore what he's saying.'

Of course I couldn't ignore it. I had grown up on cover-ups and conspiracies. In college, I had argued late into the night about who killed Kennedy. I had demonstrated against our secret war in Cambodia. I had watched in horrified fascination at the unfolding of Watergate. If the unspeakable crookedness of government was an article of radical faith, then I was a believer. Marshall was pushing on an open door.

The ferry was approaching Tower Bridge again, and we were leaving the darkness of the docklands.

'You're making quite a claim, Major,' I said.

He lit a cigarette with patience. 'Am I? Let's put it in perspective. I'm not saying that tanks will roll down Constitution Hill towards Trafalgar Square. What I'm talking about

193

is a concerted effort by a small group of hardliners to discredit the elected leaders of the country, and to persuade the voters to turn their backs on what they see as corrupt liberals and to choose a party, a leader, with more conviction.'

'Presumably on the right.'

'Presumably.'

I smiled. 'You don't seem to have gotten very far.'

'On the contrary, look at the chaos here. The worse it gets, the more the people will listen to what is being suggested.'

Then I made a remark I still regret, a remark that continues to haunt me. 'Surely you don't expect an opposition party led by a woman to be of much help to you?'

Marshall was irritated. 'Look, I'm not saying there's a blueprint. I'm not in the business of making predictions. Who knows what will happen? All I'm saying is that what I've described has happened, and the point is: it's still going on.'

'Why on earth are you telling me all this? What would your colleagues say?'

The ferry was passing under Tower Bridge, and once again the captain sent a blast on the horn reverberating through the gloomy piers.

'I've become an embarrassment to the powers that be. I'm afraid that if I don't entrust my story to an outsider it might get lost, if you see what I mean.'

'Are you offering to be a kind of Deep Throat?'

'That man was never identified. I sometimes wonder if he ever existed. My problem is that they know all about me. They may even know that we are here together now.' He seemed to enjoy the frisson. 'They know they have to watch me. They know I no longer believe in what they're doing. They know I think they've gone too far.' Marshall pointed across the water at the Tower and the riverside entrance to Traitors' Gate. 'When that place was not just a tourist attraction, what I've described would have been called high treason.'

'It can't just be that they're worried about your bad conscience?'

He shook his head. 'I went further. First of all, I refused orders. I said I was beginning to disapprove of the operation. And then . . .' He was hesitating. 'Then I told some people in another outfit, one of our rivals actually, about what was going on. I made a big miscalculation. I thought I would be safe that way. I could not have been more wrong.'

'What happened?'

'I'm being hounded by everyone. Whatever has happened behind closed doors, they all have a common interest to keep it out of the public domain, as it's called.' He threw his cigarette into the water. 'So that's why I've told you. To make it public.'

'But why me?' The question was disingenuous, but I don't apologise.

'I think you know the answer to that question.'

I looked at him hard. 'I want you to tell me.' I confess that even then I was hoping for a reprieve.

'The prime mover behind this operation is not unknown to you.'

I nodded dumbly, lost for words. I watched the water breaking on the bow and shook my head at what I had become involved in. I had come to meet Major Marshall because Ruth had asked me, but now, at the point of departure, I found I was here on my own account. I was used to a certain moral freedom: it was a shock to find myself in a position of responsibility.

'How did you discover who I was?'

He smiled, a professional on top of his work. 'Personal information, as you can appreciate, is part of my stock-in-trade. I know a great deal about your father, one way and another. As soon as Ruth mentioned your name, that day you telephoned, I guessed who you were. I thought: this may be my lucky break.'

195

I was determined to challenge him. 'But why not approach some other hack?'

'If you were to write my story, as I hope you will, then it can't be denied. Who would believe that a son could tell such lies about his father?'

I laughed. 'Fathers and sons. That's the oldest one in the book. As you well know, people will believe anything if they want to.'

'In this case they would be right to.'

'But if I did write it, as you suggest, that would be to betray him.'

'From what Ruth has told me, you wouldn't be averse to putting the boot in.' He had me on a fork, and he knew it. 'It would not be the first time that a son has avenged his mother.'

I looked at Ruth, my smiling traitor. Now I felt like the bride stripped bare. I could not deny that, in intimate moments, I had spoken harshly about my father. But this was of a different order. I was lost for words. 'Perhaps you're right,' I said.

'Anyway,' Marshall went on, implacably, 'you can't do him much harm now. He's finished. When I told the other department about Monty Python he was immediately disgraced.'

I refused to go down without a fight. 'That's the first I've heard of it.' I was on the ropes, and I knew it. 'He was given an honour in the New Year list.'

'Exactly.' Marshall nodded, as if at the definitive proof of a complicated proposition. 'Be sure of it, Seymour, he'll never serve his Queen or country again.'

Such cynicism would be typical of the establishment. It is a measure of my dismay that I did not put him straight about my name. The moment passed. To Marshall I would always be 'Seymour'. Finally I said: 'Perhaps if you're to clinch your story, you should show me your documents.'

It was a way of buying time, an opportunity for me to review my situation.

The ferry was in sight of Charing Cross Pier. In a few minutes we would be shaking hands and going our separate ways.

'I can't leave the boat in your company,' said Marshall. 'Are you free tomorrow?'

'Tomorrow's the President's last day. I'll be very busy.' I heard my eagerness to meet again with regret. 'What about Wednesday?'

'In the evening?' Marshall preferred the shadows.

'Come to my hotel. Say, nine o'clock. In my room.'

He seemed pleased. We exchanged another finger-breaking handshake. There was a bump as the ferry came alongside the pier and then shouts and the throwing of ropes. Ruth and I watched Marshall's dark shape hurry up the gangway and disappear into the night. If we were being watched, then it was done without our knowing.

I was relieved to be alone again. I put my arm around Ruth and kissed her.

'Now I know why you wanted me to meet Marshall.'

She looked up at me, smiling. 'Why's that?'

'So I have to stay here longer.'

'Do you?'

'Well,' I said, 'at the very least I'll now have to visit my father.'

9

I did not exactly lie to my wife, but I was parsimonious
with the truth. I said I had to pay my filial respects and
would be home a couple of days later than expected. If Lizzie
had suspicions, she did not speak them. She knew my feelings
about the Beaver only too well. Indeed, she shared them and
had always encouraged the idea of a rapprochement based on
what she called 'having it out'. When the phrase cropped up
again in our transatlantic conversation I could not suppress
a shameful smile at the stupid thought that I was 'having it
off' as well.

The summit was over. The captain and the kings had
departed. After the glitter of the international diplomatic
cavalcade, Air Force One had taken the Old Man back
to the domestic grindstone of tax, inflation and porkbarrel
politicking. I had asked for, and been granted, leave to see
my father. For a brief moment, I could do as I pleased.

I took a train to the West Country. It was a bright May
day with hardly a cloud in the sky. The English landscape
was a picture from a tourist brochure. How comical some
of those place-names are! Nether Wallop, Piddletrenthide,
Durdle Door, Fishpond Bottom, Walter Ralegh's Budleigh
Salterton, Ugborough, and Dawlish. I decided that 'dawlish'
was how I felt that day. At such moments I find myself
regretting my loss of British citizenship, my passport to the
shires.

I have already described my father's house in winter,
but nothing can prepare the visitor for the transformation
of early summer. Surrounded by shrubs and trees newly in
leaf and carpets of late spring flowers, the place becomes a
rural paradise. As I approached in the taxi along the rough

coast road I saw, in the distance, the orchard in blossom and a herd of cows grazing along the iron fence that separates the house from its land, and I glimpsed what it was my father would always fight to defend.

In England, such property guarantees privacy, but it also comes with ill-defined social obligations. True to form, the Beaver was complaining about his parochial duties as he came across the gravel to meet me. He was speaking in mid-sentence, as if articulating a conversation running in his head.

'. . . God made them, high or lowly, and ordered the estate to drive the rich man to wrack and ruin. Welcome.' He shook my hand with a self-deprecating laugh and I asked about his troubles.

'Our new padre is one of these sanctimonious oiks from the inner city. I was hoping to turn the church fête into a Jubilee party, but this bright spark says he's against the idea "on principle" whatever the hell that means. You wouldn't believe the amount of socialist claptrap I've had to listen to these past few weeks.'

'It would appear, from your complaint,' I said with a smile, 'that despite the priest's radicalism, he still wants you to inaugurate the occasion.'

'The villagers expect it,' he growled. 'Besides, I'd never get my fields cut if I didn't.' He turned towards the house. 'I'm planning to stir up a peasants' revolt. I shall open the fête as usual, then, before Red Robbo can stop me, I'll propose a loyal toast and get the band to play the National Anthem. It will be wonderfully embarrassing.' I could see he was enjoying the prospect. 'I'm sure you'd approve, Gilchrist. You Americans have a real penchant for the embarrassing.'

It was always 'you Americans', as if the English half of my heritage was not something he cared to acknowledge, as if those years of my childhood had been conveniently swept under the carpet. I knew better than to complain, just as I knew better than to argue with his view of Americans in general. I simply expressed what I felt: that it was a great pleasure to escape the city for a day. The summit, I added, making conversation as we went towards the house, had gone better than expected.

'You should tell your boss that he smiles too much for a world leader.' He whistled for the dog. 'If I hadn't broken bread with your mother's family I'm not sure I could make head or tail of what he's saying.'

I followed him indoors. We're not close, but I've spent enough time with him over the years to know when to ignore him and when to rise to the bait. It was too soon for an argument, and besides he was now shaking a home-made cocktail in my honour. 'Any excuse will do,' he murmured as he bent over the drinks tray. He was as charming, as dangerous and as unpredictable as ever, mellowing with age, perhaps, but still with some fairly wild ideas thrashing around inside him.

My father handed me a glass. 'This is supposed to be a Manhattan. Nice to see you. An agreeable surprise. Cheers.'

I raised my glass. 'Your good health, sir.'

He looked at me. 'Don't mention my bloody health. I'm getting on, Sam. I feel my age, dammit. I'm not the man I was.' He winked at me. 'I'm glad to see that you, however, are keeping the family traditions alive.'

'I'm not sure what you mean.' Actually, I knew perfectly well what he was alluding to.

'You were over here just a month ago, Sam. Now you're back again. Do I detect a spot of trouble in paradise?'

He had an eye for these things. I hesitated. I knew he liked Lizzie. He had, inevitably, missed our wedding, but we had made a point of visiting him together on our honeymoon.

'You know what marriage is like,' I said.

He smiled. 'I do indeed.'

'Perhaps you can give me some advice.'

'Are you in love?'

No one had asked me that question before, but then no one knew to ask. 'It feels that way,' I said.

'Love or lust?'

Now it was my turn to smile. He always went to the heart of things. 'Good question.'

I felt the warmth of his approval, a fellow player in the great game. 'What's her name?'

I told him. 'She's from Australia.'

'An affair Down Under.' He pondered his drink reflectively. 'How's your mother?'

I gave a lively account of her activities. I knew she wrote to him from time to time, but I imagined that her letters favoured a high-minded narrative of Washington life. 'I think she's happy,' I concluded. 'She says it's good to see a Democrat in the White House.'

He was only half listening. 'My life has been made by women, and unmade by them, too.'

I felt light-headed with the cocktail. 'That sounds like one of your exaggerations,' I said.

He shook his head, cutting me down to size. 'I wish you were right.' He finished his drink and stood up. 'My advice? Enjoy what you can, but don't forget your children.' He took me by the arm, as much for support as guidance. 'How is my dear little granddaughter?'

I had brought some snapshots of Alice and Charlie building a snowman in our yard. We looked at these together on the dining-room table while Jane Bell, discreet as ever, served lunch.

I say that Jane was unobtrusive, but when I think back to the occasion I recognise that she moved about the dining-room with rather more style and self-confidence than usual, as if she was the lady of the house, not the housekeeper. When she had finished serving she took her place next to my father. This was new. In the past, she had sat opposite, formal and slightly apart.

I see now that Jane needed to be near him. He was not as well as he pretended. There was a silver pill box laid by his place. Typically, he made a jocular reference to his quack doctor, but there was no laughter in his eyes as he swallowed his medicine.

I changed the subject, and asked about Susan.

'She's away on a course, a residential chamber group,' said Jane. 'She's sorry to miss you.'

'How is she?'

'Much better, thank you, at the moment,' said Jane. 'Isn't she, Ronald?'

She had never, to my recollection, addressed my father by his first name in my hearing before, and I did my best to conceal my surprise.

My father seemed embarrassed as well, and became gruffly taciturn. 'Seems to be,' he said, without enthusiasm.

I changed the subject and asked him about his recent honour, but he would not play, remarking sardonically that it was 'just another stupid gong'.

Perhaps it was the onset of illness, but after the high spirits of his greeting, he became strangely pessimistic. At one point in the conversation he looked up and said: 'If I was younger, I'd follow your example and emigrate. This country is finished.'

'If you lived in America, you'd think America was finished, too.' I knew from my mother that the country clubs of Virginia were full of old men talking fondly about Hoover and the scandals of the New Deal. 'You've reached the age when everything in the past is golden. You shouldn't write this place off just yet.'

'I'm not sure I like that suggestion.' He gave a ghost of a laugh. 'You Americans –' Now I knew his spirits were returning. 'You Americans are always telling us what to think and how to improve ourselves. That's the big difference between us, apart from our language, of course.' He poured some more wine into his glass and pushed the bottle towards me. 'Speaking of which, what is this frightful word I hear . . .'

Now he was off and running with his favourite subject,

the decline of the English language, the misuse and mispro-
nunciation of good old words, and, worst of all, the arrival,
like plague bacilli, of hideous new Americanisms into our –
it was very much 'our' – language. In his fear of American
influence abroad he was typical of his class and generation.

We argued good-naturedly for a while about the origins
of words, finished lunch and then sat in his study for coffee.
He was a great reader. The books in his library had the look
of an army used to regular exercise. I sensed that he had
something to confide.

'Jane seems well,' I said, making conversation.

The Beaver lit a cigar. 'We just got married.' He spoke
as if he was a City chairman announcing modest half-year
profits.

We have never been an emotional family. 'Congratu-
lations,' I said. I was pleased for Jane.

'You're the first to know, apart from the registrar, of
course. At my age it seems ridiculous, but . . .'

'It's a good thing to do,' I said, smiling inwardly at
the irony.

'Well, that's all right then,' he said, sarcastically. 'Finish
your coffee and give the blushing bride a kiss. Then we'll go
and see how the preparations for the bloody fête are coming
along.' He began to sing to himself, resting his feet on a low
stool. 'O death, where is thy sting-a-ling-a-ling, O grave thy
victory . . . ?'

10

We drove to the village, the three of us, in the Beaver's ancient Bentley. Now that my father had broken the news, his bride could speak more freely about their marriage and our conversation gave the old barouche a nuptial air. Jane would never throw off the habits of deference, but I was amused at the determined way she was changing the terms of their relationship. I believe her firmness, during these last years, did give him a new lease of life, while her tolerance excused the worst of his behaviour. My father was always an impossible man.

The common land in front of the church was traditionally set aside for the annual fête. It was a popular local occasion. Each spring, gypsies and small-time fairground buskers would fetch up here with their caravans and tethered dogs, to entertain and rip off the villagers. Today, mid-week, the first arrivals were staking out their territory. On Saturday, it would be a picture. Stalls set out under the stately Spanish chestnut trees that fringed the common. A crush round the Oxfam table, the tombola and the lucky dip. Mothers with small children trailing from cake stall to bring-and-buy to charity raffle. Out on the grass, people would line up to guess the weight of the pig, or take a shy at the coconuts. There would be goldfish to win, darts and hoops to throw, and fortunes to be told. Perhaps I'm sentimental, but I saw faces here that seemed to go back to the Armada, to Wat Tyler, to the Domesday Book itself. Beyond, in the churchyard, you would find their intermarried family names, Bazely, Crockett, Matthews, Parkes and Shaw, chipped into mossy headstones.

'Speaking of the English language,' said my father, as

he parked the car. 'Do you think I should write my memoirs?'

'Aren't you too busy for that?'

He glossed over the question. 'I'm pretty much a back number these days.'

I could not prevent my current obsession creeping in. 'Would you tell the truth?'

'Good God no.' He laughed. 'How could I? I would have to betray far too many confidences, but there is an authorised version I could tell that might interest people.'

'Has someone asked you?'

He became coy. 'It was Jane's idea. She says I need something to occupy my mind.'

I smiled at my new stepmother. 'I see you're getting him under control at last.'

She shook her head. 'No one will ever do that.'

We strolled across the grass together, my father in his Panama hat, cricket blazer and cravat, Jane in her floral dress. I found myself being introduced, left and right, as the American prodigal, a strategy that gave the Beaver ample opportunity to parade his opinions about the President.

Jane explained she had charity business to settle and hurried away. I saw she was taking advantage of my visit to have a little time to herself. My father was, at the best of times, a tiring companion.

The parish priest came up. He was short and bearded, with the pallid belligerence of the evangelical. He seemed anxious to confirm the arrangements for Saturday. It was plain that he did not trust my father. I listened as the Beaver taunted him with an affectation of upper-class atheism. When he became bored with the game, he terminated the conversation abruptly. 'If you'll excuse me, padre, I have to sit down.'

I noticed he was slightly out of breath. We moved on.

'A shifty bugger,' said my father, not troubling to lower his voice. 'He reminds me of a small-time rapist. What these Holy Joes never hoist in,' he went on, 'is that the way to people's imaginations is through their hearts not their consciences.'

We found a bench. I noticed with sadness the labour my father took to seat himself, but he would not be helped.

'This fellow talks of nothing but a loving God and the forgiveness of sins. How can you believe in such a thing? I've seen too much of his loving God at work to accept that line. Of course, religion has its uses. It keeps people in order and encourages respect, but that's about it.' He was still needling me. 'While we're on the subject, that President of yours goes to church too much for my liking.'

'He's sincere,' I said. 'I believe him.' These were vain words. I remembered that when I looked at my father I was looking into the face of the ultimate pragmatist. 'People are weary of cynical realpolitik.'

'They'll want cynicism soon enough when they realise their preacher President is making them poor and miserable. Voters don't want pie in the sky, they want money in the bank and bread on the table.'

'The President is an idealist. He believes in trying to do things in a new way.'

'Good luck to him.' The Beaver's intolerance was benign. 'Greed, jealousy, fear, ambition. That's what makes people tick. You can't feed a family on ideals, and you can't run a country on sermons.'

'I write those sermons.'

'And I'm sure they're brilliant, but that's beside the point. The world wants leaders, not lectures. That's the thing about power – you have to exercise it.'

'That's your philosophy. You happen to believe in power. Some of us have learnt to fear it.' In my mind's eye I saw B-52s in formation over the ricefields of Vietnam, orange and green pictures of death and destruction, a shadowy figure in an underground car park.

'I grew up with it, Sam. I've seen power from the

barrel of a gun, and with a flag in its hand. I've tried, in my way, to exercise power, and not always with success. I suppose you could say it's second nature to me now.' He prodded the turf with his stick. 'Now all I can do is watch from the sidelines and write my memoirs.'

'When Machiavelli went into exile,' I said, 'he wrote *The Prince*.'

He looked at me sharply. 'Who says I'm in exile?'

'Just a manner of speaking,' I said, waving vaguely at the wooded hills around us. 'I meant that you should use your leisure to write an analysis of power.'

The Beaver seemed amused. 'Am I such a devil?' He shook his head. 'I'm not in that league. Besides, what I'd want to write about is happening before our very eyes.' He pointed at the cheerful bustle in front of us. 'This is an idyllic scene, you might think, but behind it there is a power struggle going on, a struggle for control, for ownership. Look at that bloody priest. He's part of it. If we're not careful, we – I mean the middle classes – will end up in Trotsky's dustbin.'

'All empires decline. You can't stop the clock.'

'I don't want to stop the clock. I want to refurbish the bloody thing. More means worse, anyone can see that. What we're being threatened with is the tyranny of the mediocre, the tyranny of the many, and the government isn't doing a damn thing about it.'

'What's your answer?'

'I'm not in a position to give answers any more. I know people say I'm in sympathy with those fellows who talk about private armies, but that's utter balls. Frankly, that sort of thing is for the birds. What I will say is I have no time for compromise. Call me old-fashioned, Sam, but I've always preferred radical solutions. I sometimes think I'm too bloody romantic for the present generation.'

He was always going to be egotistical, but I was glad he

was being honest with me. In his own way, he was making his confession.

A companionable silence fell between us. We watched a class of schoolchildren practising sack-races. The Beaver entered into the sport, waving his silver-handled cane and cheering the competitors.

'It's funny, sitting here together like this,' I said, during a lull in the excitement. 'I used to hate you. When I was first away at school in Washington, I used to stick pins into my teddy bear and pretend it was you.'

'I'm not surprised,' he said. 'I didn't behave very well. I believe I've made it up with your mother now, in a way. I hope so.' He turned towards me, half humorous. 'You have also grown up to be unfaithful,' he said. 'Now you've betrayed Lizzie perhaps I'll be next.'

I sensed his meaning, even if I did not exactly understand him. 'I think I'd always be afraid to,' I replied.

'You'll find a way,' He was almost daring me. He wanted me to be his son, to live dangerously and behave badly. I was not ready then, though I have discovered I am ready now. The irony is that it's too late to prove myself to him.

'I suppose I would,' I wanted to say, 'if I thought it would help my mother, I would betray you. If it was one of those choices they put in films, if I had to choose between one parent and another, I would sacrifice you.'

I didn't say any of that, but I thought it. What I actually said was: 'If I was to betray you, you'd first have to put yourself in my power.'

He smiled. 'Well, perhaps I'm about to do that.' He saw the puzzlement in my face. 'I want you to be my executor.' He stood up. 'If you come back with me to the house, I'll show you what that might involve.'

He sounded casual, but he must have known that he was about to dive into deep waters. Did he miscalculate his reserves of sangfroid? Did he, in retrospect, regret this invitation? That was the day on which, for the first and last time in my life, I saw my father cry.

11

My father had married Jane at last, but many bachelor habits remained. He slept alone. His bedroom at the top of the stairs was just as I remembered it, the narrow bed, wardrobe and cluttered escritoire.

He sat at the desk. I sat on the bed, on the cool bedspread. Faintly, through the open window, we could hear the village band rehearsing 'Hello, Dolly'. As he organised his papers, I looked about me.

The room was a museum to a lifetime of foreign adventure. The tall willow-pattern vases flanking the fireplace came from China. The brassbound wooden trunk at the foot of the bed had once been roped to the back of an elephant. The rug by the door had been woven high on the North-West Frontier. The mask on the wall was from West Africa, a present from an Ashanti chief. I believe there are rooms like this all over England, unexpected nests of colonial souvenirs.

'Perhaps you should write your memoirs,' I said. 'I'd forgotten what a life you've had.'

'I miss it,' he replied, not looking round. 'I used to love packing my bag. Now . . . ' He seemed lost for words, as if unable or unwilling to acknowledge that he was finally grounded.

'I guess,' I went on, trying to find a note of sympathy, 'those opportunities just don't exist any more. I mean, imperialism is out of fashion.' I heard myself talking like what the English call a prig and I stopped.

My father was turning an ivory statuette over in his fingers, only half listening. 'This came from Biafra. The chap who gave it to me is almost certainly dead now, poor fellow.' He was silent for a moment, and then caught up

210

with my words. 'Imperialism? You're full of isms, Sam. Is that all they teach you in college these days?'

'Academics like isms,' I said. 'Isms are good for business.'

The Beaver was looking into the middle distance. 'I do believe that when historians look back on what we did they will say that we were rather brilliant imperialists. Not a master race, but a masterly one.' I did not interrupt. He was thinking aloud. 'Why on earth should a British engineer and his family settle in the blazing bush to devote his life to making the railway run smoothly to Timbuctoo or Lake Victoria? The truth is that those colonial adminis-trators believed in what they were doing, and what's more they had the courage to act on their beliefs. Brave men with fire in their bellies. That's half our trouble nowadays, we've no conviction any more, no vision.'

I didn't agree, of course. As a former student of Marx and Lenin, it was impossible. As a son I kept my thoughts to myself. His masterly conviction was my high-handed oppression. So long as I refused to be drawn by this pre-posterous, complacent nonsense, I would keep my temper and the day would not be spoiled. We weren't here to debate politics, we were here to look at his papers.

I said: 'Convictions can be dangerous things.'

He had opened the desk-top and was taking out a govern-ment-issue manila envelope. 'You may be more right than you realise,' he said, 'but let's agree that chaos in society is just as dangerous.'

On this occasion, I was happy to concede.

'For what it's worth,' he went on, in a better humour, 'my convictions have never done me much good.' He handed me the envelope. It was bulging with papers, but sealed. It was addressed to me, in spidery writing, Seymour J. Lefevre Esq., a.k.a. Mr Sam Gilchrist – a truly Anglo-American hybrid. 'These papers,' he said, as I weighed the packet in my hand, 'will go some way to explain why I am reluctant to write my memoirs. They will also entrust to

211

you the care of your half-sister, my daughter Susan.' He smiled reassuringly. 'Don't look so alarmed. You are both reasonably well provided for.' The smile became a frown. 'Whatever the specialists pretend, she will always need professional care.'

I had supposed these papers contained the details to which Marshall had referred, but he seemed to be saying that they were rather more personal. 'I'll do what I can,' I said. 'She's had a raw deal.'

At another time, such a hint of censure might have provoked an angry reaction. Today, he just stared pathetically at his desk. 'Sometimes,' he said, 'I wish I had acknowledged her sooner. Then, perhaps, there would have been no crisis.'

'You could not have known,' I said. 'You should not blame yourself.'

An expression of sadness passed across his face. 'In my blacker moments, I wish she had never been born.' He put his hand to his eyes in a gesture of defeat. 'Is that a terrible thing to admit?'

I was at a loss to know how to answer. Against my will, I found myself feeling sorry for the old man. He had lived life to the full, according to his convictions, and life had let him down. Now he was too deep into his own remorse to be within the reach of my sympathy.

I said, hopefully, 'I also have my black moments.'

He hardly seemed to hear me. He was humming to himself, a tune from Gilbert and Sullivan, I think, a mannerism that was usually the preamble to a reminiscence.

'After your mother took you back to the United States, I had many affairs. My life, in retrospect, fell to pieces. I did not love Jane – not really – but I've come to love her. What saved me was Susan, my darling daughter. She was growing into an enchanting little girl and I was becoming more and more devoted to her. I regret to say she had no real idea who I was. The fact is that we lied to her. I can't think what possessed us, unless it was shame. It was a terrible mistake.'

'How did she know you?'

'As an old friend of her mother's. I was her Uncle Ronnie. Absurd, isn't it?'

'I don't know. It probably seemed right at the time.'

'When she was twelve years old, she and her mother moved here, as you know.'

I nodded. I had left grad school by then, and Lizzie was expecting Alice.

'That was when I told your mother at last. And then she, I believe, explained the situation to you.'

'I remember it well,' I said. 'Mother was afraid I would resent the cover-up, but actually I was pleased to find I had a sister.'

The wind had got up and was blowing the papers about. The room seemed chill. I went over and closed the window. Outside, the band had stopped and clouds were filling the sky from the west.

The best and worst times in life never leave us. I can recall exactly the moment my mother first told me about Susan. It was at home in Georgetown. We were sitting at our kitchen table after brunch one Sunday. Outside, it was a bright spring day, full of promise. Lizzie had taken Charlie to the park in his buggy. Mother had cried a little, a proud, lonely woman with all her illusions taken from her. I was torn: angry on her behalf, but happy for myself. I was not alone any more. I had a sister, or a sort of a sister. I had no idea, then, how soon her unsettled mind would spin her out of my reach.

I looked at my father now. He was leaning on the desk, the evidence of his life arraigned before him, but somehow unable to pass sentence. He seemed old and hollow and no longer dangerous.

'What went wrong?' I asked.

'We'll probably never know exactly,' he said. 'I believe it was the shock of what we told her, but the doctors say you cannot be sure.' He shrugged. 'There are no excuses. I

213

should have seen the signs, and so should Jane. God knows why we sent her away to boarding school. She was rather shy and withdrawn and I suppose we thought, in our misguided way, that the experience would be character-forming.'

'In America we can never understand why the English do this to their children.'

'Or themselves,' said my father. 'No one was more miserable than Jane when Susan went away.' He cleared his throat, a butler announcing an uninvited guest. 'I was up in town when the call came from the headmistress. Your daughter has tried to commit suicide. She is suffering from an acute adolescent breakdown.' He paused. 'Of course, we hurried to the school as fast as we could. One look at her was enough for me. She was quite beyond reach.' I had never seen him moved as he was now. 'She's better at the moment, but she comes and goes. She'll never be the same again. You could say that I lost her as soon as I had found her. I believe that's what drove me mad.'

For the first time, I was beginning to see the logic of Marshall's story, and I felt a surge of curiosity. 'How do you mean?'

'I was commuting to Belfast at the time. A spot of troubleshooting. My task was to sort out some inter-service rivalry. A routine assignment. Suddenly I found myself in utter desperation, and no one to talk to. My daughter was in psychiatric care. My life made no sense.' He broke off. He had gone too far. 'Look, I don't usually talk about these things, and God knows when I'm going to see you again, but –'

'I can keep a secret,' I said.

It was the right answer. 'Good.' He seemed relieved. 'What I'm telling you now I have never revealed to a single living soul.' He smiled, coming out of himself. 'My generation thought it bad form to talk about oneself.'

'Your generation is like all generations,' I said, 'totally fucked up.'

He laughed then, and so did I, deep, cleansing laughter that made me light-headed and even glad. For once in my life I was speaking to my father as a fellow human being. He took out a large white handkerchief and dabbed the tears from his eyes, hardly knowing, I think, if he was experiencing sadness or joy.

'Look,' he said, when he had composed himself again. He began tearing open the envelope with my name on it. Photographs, memos and newspaper clippings spilled onto the desk. 'If I show you this stuff now, then we can both forget about it.'

At his invitation, and with some nervousness, I shuffled the documents. Many were marked 'Top Secret'. In the space of a few minutes, it was impossible to grasp the details, but from what I had already heard from Marshall, the overall picture was clear enough. Here was the official record of my father with government ministers and Army officers, of men in suits going in and out of buildings, the dark underside of the state. Mixed in with these grey images were fuzzy, compromising photographs, presumably snatched by hidden cameras, of men, perhaps the same men, in various states of undress, with women, with boys, and with themselves alone. It was not, as they say, a pretty sight.

We did not speak. After some minutes, I looked up. 'I'm glad you've showed me this,' I said, 'but it doesn't make much sense to me.'

'Frankly,' he said, 'it never made much sense. But I was in this mood. I felt trapped. I wanted to destroy the world I was living in and this seemed as good a place to start as any.'

'I think I know what you mean,' I said. 'It can be an exhilarating feeling.'

'It's easy to say this now, but we got carried away.'

'So you were not alone?' I wondered, as I said this, if Marshall's name would come up.

'Good God, no. We were quite a shooting party. I was

215

probably the most extreme. I felt I had nothing to lose. This was during the worst of Susan's illness, before they got her medication right. I probably needed help, too. Jane says that subconsciously I wanted to disgrace myself.' He smiled. 'I certainly succeeded.'

I tried to strike a positive note. 'At least it seems you are now reconciled to yourself.'

He shrugged. 'What happened, happened. There's nothing to be gained from having regrets. As you might expect, my superiors prefer it that way.'

In my dealings with British government officials, I've noticed that they like to let sleeping dogs lie. I saw Marshall facing upriver on the Greenwich ferry, lonely and implacable. He was not playing the game, or at any rate he did not understand the rules. He would pay for that. I looked at my father and smiled. 'For a troublemaker you're rather docile.'

'Never complain, never explain, that's my motto.' This was the authentic voice of my father in his prime. 'So much for the documents. We can recce my last will and testament over dinner. Nothing like as much fun as this stuff.'

The subject was closed. As I have related, he never willingly referred to it again in his lifetime, and it was part of the unspoken pact between us that I should honour this silence. Craig Marshall's subsequent interventions were all the more unwelcome for that reason.

Now my father pushed the incriminating papers together and pulled his old wicker waste-paper basket towards him. With what appeared to be second thoughts, he rescued a photograph of himself and Harold Wilson inspecting a line of troops from the pile.

'Funny,' he said. 'Despite everything, I rather liked him. I'll keep that.' He put the print among the family portraits on the top of the desk, an incongruous relative. Then he shovelled all the other papers into the bin.

He stood up, holding the trash basket in his hand like a

prisoner with a slop pail. 'I know I can trust you,' he said, putting his finger to his lips.

He pointed to the folder with O'Reilly's papers. 'Bring that with you, dear boy. You can browse it at your leisure, and while I remember it, when I kick the bucket I want no funeral orations. I've heard enough official lying to last well beyond the grave. You will promise me that, won't you?'

'I promise,' I said.

12

In the Palm Court of the Waldorf Hotel there was music
and laughter, but I was in no mood for either. I waited in
my hotel room, alone. Here, at least, I had kept my word.
I was on time. I had taken the evening train and reached
London just as the light was going. The summer sun sets
so slowly in England.

Ruth was late, as usual. I ordered room service, first one,
then a second, then a third cocktail. I looked at my watch.
The time was crawling by. Nine-thirty, nine-thirty-five,
nine-forty . . .

This was my last night in London. Tomorrow I would fly
home to my family in a whirl of duplicity and self-doubt. In
my search for certainty, something I could trust and believe
in, I wanted these last hours with Ruth. We should go to a
show, enjoy a quiet dinner, and then share a night of love.
(We, who write words for a mass audience, are used to the
images of mass consumption.) Yet here I was watching some
brainless TV sitcom, waiting for a knock at the door and
a visit from a middle-aged man with a dubious hard-luck
story and a chip on his shoulder. Perhaps if I could dispose
of him quickly there would still be time for dancing.

'Come on, Marshall,' I said out loud.

I was lolling on the bed with a glass in my hand when I
heard a click, and then a footfall. I got up in a hurry, feeling
vulnerable. Marshall's shadow filled the room. 'Hi,' I said.

'Hello there.' He seemed nervous and out of breath, and
I guessed he had just walked up several flights of stairs to
avoid the elevator. He was carrying a Civil Service briefcase
and would have passed, in the street, for a homebound commuter. 'I could use a drink.'

I handed him the room service menu and he studied it like a route map. 'You know, Seymour,' he said, 'I think I'd love the States.' He was murmuring to himself, 'Manhattan, Screwdriver, Rusty Nail, Harvey Wallbanger . . .' He paused and looked up. 'I'll have a Jack Daniel's,' he said, with relish.

I picked up the phone and rang through the order. 'Room 303. Two Jack Daniel's on the rocks.' As I was speaking, I saw Marshall out of the corner of my eye checking out my suite – lounge, bedroom, bathroom, and wardrobe.

I put the phone down. 'Okay?'

'Okay.' He went over and switched on the bedside radio. 'You can't be too careful.' He sat down in the armchair by the window, collecting himself and looking about warily.

We chatted idly for some minutes, both conscious of killing time. I explained that Ruth was on her way. He made a crack about her punctuality, but I did not smile. I did not like the assumption of familiarity behind Marshall's comment. On the radio, they were playing 'Knowing Me, Knowing You'.

There was a knock on the door. We both started. Marshall's jumpiness was infectious. As I signed for the drinks I found myself wondering about the waiter's identity. We watched him go in silence. Then I checked that the corridor was deserted and dropped the 'Do Not Disturb' sign. I came back into my room, with the drink singing in my veins.

Marshall was standing by the bed. He had picked up the Gideon Bible. I watched as he flipped the pages. He seemed lost. 'When I was a lad,' he said, 'we went to church every Sunday, Presbyterian of course. And then Sunday school.' He put the bible down. 'I still go occasionally.'

'Old habits die hard,' I said.

'No.' He shook his head vigorously in a way I came to know as typical. 'There must be a God.'

I might have guessed that he would have a religious

219

disposition. In an earlier century, he would have set off to besiege the Infidel, a loyal crusader obeying orders. In his own career, he had trusted his superiors and they had let him down. His was the fury of the much-deceived.

'Onward Christian soldiers,' I said, smiling to hide my embarrassment.

He looked at me reproachfully and laid the bible aside. 'Let's get down to business.' He put his briefcase on the bed and began to unpack a set of buff folders. 'In the States, my case would be a cause célèbre. Look at Watergate. That should be our model. Everything's a cover-up here.'

He was still laying out his exhibits like a travelling salesman when the door opened without warning. We both turned, guilty men fearing a sting. It was Ruth. She came in, wet-haired and blithe as ever. She skipped over to kiss me. I tasted the faint bite of chlorine on her lips. I hugged her close, but she broke free and kissed Marshall too. I went over and locked the door, pretending not to care.

We returned to Marshall's papers in earnest. All three of us were now sitting on the bed. Ruth was enjoying the incongruity. 'I always wanted three in a bed,' she remarked, lying back on the pillow.

'These are photocopies of course,' said Marshall, sternly reminding us of our purpose.

The folders had labels, '1973', '1974', 'Monty Python', '1975', and so on. I realised, as Marshall began to elaborate his story, that I had seen some of these papers only yesterday, with my father.

My attention wandered. Marshall was explaining the details of the operation. His professional pride in its technical proficiency was fighting with his dismay at its consequences. There was no mistaking his conviction, his certainty in the rightness of his cause.

I wanted to say: You've got it wrong. These documents have nothing to do with politics and the state, they are about one sad old man and his daughter.

Occasionally, to play my part, I would ask a question, but my heart was not in it. After a while, Marshall said: 'I'll have another Jack Daniel's now, thank you.'

When the waiter knocked, I took the tray from him at the door. As I handed Marshall his drink he said: 'Ruth tells me I can trust you.'

I looked at Ruth. How on earth could she know? 'Sure,' I said. 'Whatever.'

Marshall seemed pleased, as though something had been settled. He took his glass to the armchair by the window and began leafing through the Gideon Bible again. 'Listen to this, Seymour. Revelation, one, three. "Blessed is he that readeth, and they that hear the words of this prophecy, and keep those things which are written therein: for the time is at hand." ' He snapped the book shut. 'There you are. My text. My prediction.'

'I'm not a believer,' I said.

'No matter,' he replied. 'What I have written, I have written.'

'What have you written, for Christ's sake?'

'Something you don't believe –'

'What's that?'

'– and something Americans cannot understand.' He laid the book down. 'The English are looking for greatness again. If they can't have it, they'll invent it. That's the story I'm asking you to tell, the story of Monty Python.'

'Rule Britannia,' I said, ironically raising my glass.

Now, with the Union Jack flying over Port Stanley, I recall my flippancy with shame.

He was standing over me. For reasons that are only clear with hindsight, he was desperate to enlist my support. 'You won't forget what I've told you? You will help me?'

'Well,' I said, feeling drunk and insincere, 'I suppose I made you a promise.'

'A promise is a promise,' he replied, 'in any language.' He put out his hand and I shook it. I had no choice.

221

He looked at his watch. 'I must be off.' When he had finished packing his briefcase, he tore a sheet of paper from the notepad by the bedside. He was scribbling an address and telephone number. 'Stay in touch,' he said. 'Be careful.'

I watched him kiss Ruth goodbye. We shook hands once more. Then he slipped out of the door into the anonymous corridor. I wondered if I would ever see him again.

After Marshall had gone, we sat in silence together. The buzz of night traffic mixed with the muffled sounds of the hotel. My throat was dry and I was feeling hot with tiredness. I went to the minibar and cracked open a lager. Ruth was lolling on the bed. She was holding the Gideon Bible. 'Look,' she said, 'he's inscribed it. "Good luck, Seymour",' she read, ' "Revelation, one, three." '

'I suppose it had to be Revelation,' I said, noting the cramped ferocity of Marshall's signature.

Ruth was watching me. 'He's put a spell on you.'

'Don't be silly.' I didn't feel as light as I hoped. 'Anyway, no one will listen.'

'You must know someone who'd be interested.'

'I know you,' I said.

She shook her head. 'I'm a freelance. I have no reputation. You need someone with clout.'

I knew only too well what she meant. I could see those familiar faces in the media watering holes of Washington and New York, the faces you glimpse on the screen during a presidential press conference, the faces of the American inquisition, probing, sallow, unrelenting, self-satisfied. There was, they assumed, no whiff of corruption, no hint of conspiracy or scandal, they could not sniff out and expose. Perhaps they were right, in their own backyard. They believed in the shadowy figure in the underground car park.

What Marshall had to say was different. Here was a dark, tortuous story from a country they preferred to know as a kitsch symbol of a past that may never have existed. England was a place to buy antiques, a land of country-house hotels, funny accents and cream teas, a rambling drive from Windsor, via Stratford, to Bath and Wells, an airstrip from which to visit Europe. It was not a place you went looking for plots and secrets, not any more. From an American perspective, England did not count in the scheme of things, its local dramas were no longer significant.

I could imagine the journalists I knew shrug and say: 'Amazing, Sam, but it doesn't amount to a hill of beans.' Then I would riposte that I thought it was important and they would say, more truly than they could possibly realise, 'Well, you would, wouldn't you?' Everyone knew about my mixed bloodline.

'I'm doubtful,' I said. Perhaps when I got home I would run the whole thing past Lizzie, but I kept that thought to myself.

'If you want to do it, you will,' said Ruth.

In some obscure way, she interpreted my response to Marshall's story as a response to her, and I didn't realise, in my tiredness, that she was testing my feelings. 'I'm not sure that I do,' I said.

'Thanks, mate,' she said. 'Thanks a fucking million.'

I came over and pulled her up into my arms. She began to cry. I was shocked. I had not seen her tears before. 'Hold me,' she said, and then kissed me hard on the mouth. I could taste the salt in her tears and feel the desperation in the grip of her fingers.

'I'll come back,' I whispered. 'I promise.'

She pulled away from me, tears becoming anger. 'You men are so arrogant. Why does it always have to be about you?' She shook her head. 'You'll never understand, will you?'

If only I had known then what I know now. I should have realised that she did not trust herself with me, and longed for me to make a claim. She was at war inside and

223

these were tears of frustration and disappointment.

The next time she cried in my presence there was sea salt on her lips and our time was up.

'I love you,' I said.

I held her in my arms, and the tears came into her eyes, as though smarting at some hidden pain. 'Don't say that, please don't say that.'

'Why not?'

'Don't you see, Sam, it's too late.'

'Is there nothing I can do?'

'But it's not you – it's your father,' she said, sobbing without control.

I stared at her wildly.

'I tried to warn you,' she said, 'but you didn't listen.'

Her face was flushed and blotchy with tears. I felt stupid and utterly betrayed. The remorseless surf was pounding in the distance.

'I couldn't stop myself,' she said. 'I'm sorry I lied to you, but life is short and then you die. Forgive me.'

'Do you love him?' I did not know what else to say.

'I don't know what love is,' she said. 'That's my trouble.'

This was the moment when my own freedom was all I wanted, even though I had no immediate use for it.

I remember digging my fingers into the hot sand and wishing I could be buried in it forever. 'Driving on empty,' I whispered, and I wondered if I should not break down and cry myself. I realised then that we would never reach Santiago de Compostela, we would never complete the pilgrim's road.

No, if only I had known then what, to my cost, I know now. . . . When she stood before me in the hotel that night, all I wanted was reconciliation. 'I'll do anything to try,' I said.

'You'd better,' she warned. When she saw my dismay she laughed and kissed me, carefree again. In some ways she was the most completely adult person I've known, worldly, determined and sensual, and yet her mood could shift like a child's.

I began to spin a fantasy about our lives, the places we could meet and the things we could do together. When was she coming to the States? She didn't know, and I sensed that she disliked the question. She became restless.

'Let's go out,' she said.

I looked at my watch. It was nearly midnight. I yawned.

'I have to walk,' she said. 'I have to get some air. I'll be back in fifteen.'

I did not go after her, I did not even move. I heard her running feet thump down the corridor, and then the ping of the elevator. I sat down in the chair Craig Marshall had so recently vacated. I held the bible in my hands. Now that he had written in it, I would have to keep it.

'In the beginning . . .'

I remember wondering when I, too, would have the courage to begin. Shakespeare says that conscience makes cowards of us all, but, in the end, conscience can also make us brave. I speak as my father's son, but I also speak for myself.

AUTHOR'S NOTE

A novel based on a story torn from the pages of a newspaper will always have an air of reality, but Operation Monty Python is, of course, imaginary, as are the characters, English or American.

I gratefully acknowledge the following sources: *Keeping the Faith* by Jimmy Carter (New York, 1982); *Smear!, Wilson and the Secret State* by Stephen Dorril and Robin Ramsay (London 1991); 'The Passionless Presidency' by James Fallows (*The Atlantic*, Boston, April 1979); *Who Framed Colin Wallace?* by Paul Foot (London, 1989); *Bunch of Five* by Frank Kitson (London, 1977); *James E. Carter, Chronology, Documents, Bibliographical Aids*, edited by George J. Lankevich (New York, 1981); *What I Saw at the Revolution* by Peggy Noonan (New York, 1989); *England's Dreaming, Sex Pistols and Punk Rock* by Jon Savage (London, 1991); *A Very Human President* by Jack Valenti (New York, 1975).